Slowly, but surely,
his hands pushed her away

"Stacy," he whispered in agony. "What am I doing? I'm destroying both of us." He turned away, his profile hardening into an unrelenting silhouette in the starlight. "God help me, I can't let you go. I'll never let you go!"

"Cord, I don't want to go," Stacy murmured huskily. "I only want you to stop shutting me out. I want to share in your life."

A dark eyebrow arched with bitter cynicism. "What is there for me to share? My wheelchair? It's my prison, yet I'm your jailer. I'll never let you go free."

Stacy's protest was lost in the swish of his wheels as he turned away.

JANET DAILEY

For Bitter Or Worse

Harlequin Books

TORONTO • NEW YORK • LONDON
AMSTERDAM • PARIS • SYDNEY • HAMBURG
STOCKHOLM • ATHENS • TOKYO • MILAN

This edition published September 1990
ISBN 0-373-83215-X

Harlequin Presents edition published January 1979
Janet Dailey Treasury edition 1985

Original hardcover edition published in 1978
by Mills & Boon Limited

Printed in U.S.A.

CHAPTER ONE

STACY PAUSED at the opened bedroom door. Her fingers nervously smoothed the side of her hair pulled sleekly back in a clasp at the nape of her neck. A faintly medicinal scent tinged the air as she gazed around the empty room, masculine in its decor.

The house was quiet in the early-morning stillness. Distantly Stacy heard the soft bustle of Maria preparing breakfast. Anxiously her brown eyes, moving swiftly to search the living room, swept the foyer. They stopped at the sight of a wheelchair sitting in front of the veranda doors.

An achingly familiar dark head was resting against the chair back. Black hair in waving disarray glistened in the soft light of full dawn. The man in the chair sat unmoving in front of the window.

A quivering sigh trembled through Stacy. It was barely morning and Cord was already staring silently out the window. It promised to be another one of those days. There had been so many of them lately it was becoming difficult to remember the good days.

Thank goodness Josh was staying with Mary and her boys for a couple of days, Stacy thought with weary relief. Cord's black moods were beginning to take their toll on their son no matter how Stacy tried to shield Josh from them. Unbidden, the admission came that her own nerves were strained to the point of rawness.

Her brown eyes darkened with anguish at the sight of the once proud and vital man confined to a wheelchair. She felt the mental torture and pain almost as intensely as her husband did. Worst of all to bear was her inability to help him.

As if he sensed her presence, a large hand gripped a wheel and pivoted the chair around. Hurriedly Stacy fixed a bright smile on her lips before she was impaled on the rapier thrust of Cord's dark gaze.

"Good morning, darling," she murmured smoothly. "You're up and about early today."

"Yes," was Cord's harshly clipped response.

He propelled the chair forward at her approach. His clean-cut features were rigidly drawn in forbidding lines. As Stacy bent to kiss him, Cord averted his head slightly and her lips were scraped by the roughness of his lean cheek covered by a shadowy day's growth of beard. His continuous rejection of any display of affection from her cut to the quick, but Stacy tried to conceal it.

"You forgot to shave this morning," she chided laughingly, and stepped behind his chair to push him into the dining room.

"I didn't forget. I just didn't see the need," he replied tautly.

"You haven't kissed a sheet of sandpaper lately or you might change your mind about that." The forced attempt at light humor made her voice sound brittle.

"No one is making you do it, Stacy."

Cord sounded so cold and insensitive that she had to close her eyes to remember that he really loved her. It was only his bitterness talking. She couldn't blame him for being bitter.

"No one is making me," she agreed, keeping the tone of lightness, however artificial it was. "I do it strictly out of desire."

She pushed his chair to the head of the table, already set for breakfast. As she released his wheelchair handles and stepped to the seat at his right, she felt the slash of his gaze.

"Since when did my passionate wife become satisfied with a mere kiss on the cheek?" Cord jeered softly.

Stacy flinched inwardly. "It's enough for the time being." She reached for the juice pitcher sitting in the middle of the table. "It won't be forever."

His mouth quirked cynically, and something sharp stabbed Stacy's heart at the action. Maria's appearance with the coffee forestalled any caustic response Cord intended to make.

"Breakfast will be ready in a few minutes," Maria announced, filling the coffee mugs and setting the pot on the table.

"Fine," Stacy smiled, using the break to change the conversation as the plump Mexican woman left the room. "Travis will be in shortly," she told Cord. "We want to go over the yearling list with you to get your recommendations on the ones we should keep as breeding prospects."

"Spare me a token involvement." His lips thinned, hardening his expression. "You and

Travis have very capably operated the ranch this past year without my help or advice. I don't need any magnanimous gestures implying I still have a hand in running things."

Stacy's control snapped, pain bursting through her chest. Pressing her lips tightly together, she tried to breathe deeply. She couldn't endure another bitter argument.

"Cord, please. Let's not get into this again," she begged tautly.

"Then don't patronize me!" he snapped.

"We aren't," she protested.

"Aren't you?" Dark eyes flashed like burning coals. "Go over the list of yearlings," he mocked sarcastically. "The Circle H is your ranch. Do what you like!"

"It was your ranch. It became our ranch, but it was never mine," Stacy cried out in frustration. "All Travis and I have been trying to do is keep it going until—"

"—Until I was well again?" Cord interrupted, a sardonic dryness in his tone. A contemptuous sound came from his throat. "It's very likely that I'm as well as I'm going to get."

"No."

But it was a whispered word, half choked by an invisible stranglehold around her throat.

"Face the truth, Stacy," he demanded harshly, "it would have been better if Colter hadn't pulled me from the wreckage of the plane."

"How can you say that!" she breathed in sharply. Her hands were trembling. She stared at them, remembering the agony she had suffered nearly a year ago when she had thought Cord might not live. "I love you. How could you possibly think anything would be better if you were dead?"

"Look at me." When she didn't immediately obey his orders, his fingers dug into the bones of her slender wrist and twisted it until her widened brown eyes met the chilling darkness of his. There was an arrogant flare of his nostrils in challenge.

"Look at me, Stacy, and tell me if it's love you feel or pity."

Stacy obeyed, slowly inspecting his masculine features. A year's convalescence had paled his sun-browned skin to a golden hue. The chiseled lines were blunted by a weight loss that hadn't been completely regained. Yet the rugged leanness only seemed to increase his compelling looks. Marriage had not lessened the physical attraction Cord held for her, only heightened it.

There was nothing about his handsome face to pity, nor the wide shoulders and strong arms. But when her gaze slipped to his long, muscled legs that had once enabled him to tower over her, Stacy was forced to remember that Cord sat in a wheelchair.

Her heart cried at the injustice of it. It was like seeing a noble savage, proud and arrogant and chained against his will.

Yes, it tore at her heart, but it did so because she loved him.

"I love you, Cord," she answered at last, lifting her gaze to his face.

He sighed heavily and released her wrist. His hand closed around the juice glass. There was a suppressed violence about him, as if he wanted to hurl the glass and see it shatter into a thousand pieces.

Stacy laid a hand on his forearm and felt him stiffen at her touch. "Cord, you have to believe you'll walk again." She leaned toward him earnestly. "It isn't as if you're without hope. This last operation, you did regain some feeling in your legs. It's just a slow healing process until the doctors can test how extensive the recovery will be."

His hard gaze shifted to her with lazy cynicism. "Or how limited," he reminded her dryly. "Forgive me if I'd rather prepare for the worst," he mocked, shrugging his arm away from her touch.

He released the brake in his wheelchair and pushed it away from the table. "Tell Maria that I'm not hungry."

"Cord, you have to eat!" Stacy protested as he rolled toward the living room.

"I don't *have* to do anything," he replied without a backward glance.

Stacy started to follow him, then sat back in her chair. Their somewhat embittered discussion had stolen her appetite, too.

It revealed so much of the frustration they had known in the past year since the engine of Cord's plane had failed on takeoff from a friend's ranch and he had crashed.

Her own father had been killed in an air crash of a private plane, which Stacy had survived. The memory of that had been vivid when Stacy had flown to San Antonio, uncertain whether Cord would be dead or alive when she arrived. Even when she got there, it was days before the doctors felt confident about his recovery.

Their immediate concern had been stopping the internal bleeding and making the necessary repairs to keep him alive.

The operation to relieve the pressure on the main nerve trunk to his legs had been too delicate and complicated to attempt in his critical and weakened condition following the crash, so the decision had been made to wait until he had recovered his strength before attempting it.

At the time, Stacy had been too grateful to have him alive to risk losing him on the operating table, so she had agreed with the medical opinion.

Given a second chance, Stacy knew she would make the same decision. The operation to relieve the pressure had been performed only a short time ago.

It was successful to the point that he now had some feeling in his legs, although he hadn't regained the use of them.

That, the doctors felt, would depend on the body's healing process, which required time and hope. For Cord, hope was becoming threadbare from overuse. He could no longer hold on to it with any certainty that it would be fulfilled.

After being an invalid for nearly a year, his patience was gone. He had expected immediate results from the operation. Numbed legs instead of no feeling had not given him enough

encouragement. After living a life that demanded physical exertion of all sorts, Cord
faced the looming prospect of limited activity
with growing bitterness. In this bitterness, he
lashed out at everyone, and most especially
Stacy.

If he was trying to break her tenacious hold
on hope, she wondered how long she would be
able to hold on to it under his attacks. The
strain of the last months was wearing on her,
too. Sighing, she reached for the coffee.

"Stacy?" A male voice questioningly called
her name with quiet concern.

She sensed he must have spoken before, only
she hadn't heard him. She glanced up and
smiled at the dark-haired man standing beside
the table. It was a haunted smile, a ghost of the
animated warmth that it usually carried.

"Hello, Travis. I'm afraid I didn't hear you
come in," Stacy apologized, gesturing toward
a chair opposite hers. "Have some coffee."

"I saw Cord out on the veranda. Isn't he
coming with us?"

Travis McCrea sat down, smoothing a sil-
vered wing in his otherwise dark hair.

Maria walked in carrying the breakfast
plates for Stacy and Cord, enabling Stacy to
avoid Travis's question for the time being.

Maria frowned at the empty space at the head of the table and glanced at Stacy.

"Where is Mister Cord?"

"He's out on the veranda. He said he wasn't hungry, but why don't you take him a tray in case he changes his mind," Stacy suggested, knowing Cord would probably leave the food to sit or feed it to Cajun, the German shepherd.

Maria agreed, clicking her tongue as she hurried back toward the kitchen. "He will never be strong again if he doesn't eat."

Stacy sighed, drawing Travis's brown gaze. Perceptively he noticed the slight droop to her shoulders. There were faint shadows beneath her eyes and a trembling line to her mouth.

"Has he let loose already this morning?" Travis inquired gently.

"Yes," she nodded with a wry twist of her mouth.

There was no point in lying or in pretending that she didn't know what Travis was talking about. He had known Cord much longer than she had. He had even been there when Cord was pulled from the plane wreckage.

At the time Travis had been the foreman for Colter Langston, Cord's best friend and best man at their wedding.

And Travis had been the one who had met Stacy at the San Antonio airport and driven her to the hospital where Cord had been taken.

A few days after the accident, he had stopped by the hospital. It was then that Travis had told her he had quit his job with Colter and was striking out for parts unknown.

Stacy had never delved into the precise reason that Travis had left after working so many years for Colter, although she had her suspicions. Aware that Cord's convalescence would be a long one, without being aware how long, Stacy has asked Travis if he would temporarily fill the post as foreman on the Circle H until Cord was able to take over again. Almost a year later, he was still here, temporarily filling in.

"I suppose I should be used to Cord's outbursts of frustration by now," Stacy rubbed a hand across her forehead, a gesture of mental tiredness.

"No one ever gets used to it," answered Travis.

"I suppose not," she sighed.

Maria walked through the dining room with an attractively set breakfast tray for Cord. The fluffy omelet on her own plate didn't arouse Stacy's appetite, but she began eating it anyway. There was too much to be done this morning to attempt to accomplish it on an empty stomach.

The sound of the sliding glass doors opening to the veranda was heard, and unconsciously Stacy tensed as Maria's shoes clattered onto the cobblestoned veranda.

The musical lilt of Maria's voice speaking in her slightly accented English was carried into the dining room, although her exact words were not distinguishable.

There wasn't any difficulty understanding Cord.

"Dammit! I told her I wasn't hungry!" His angrily shouted words were followed by a resounding crash as the breakfast tray was obviously hurled away. "Maria, I—" This time there was a faint apologetic tone in his voice, but Cord didn't complete the sentence.

Tears burned the back of Stacy's brown eyes. Her gaze ricocheted away from the grim line of Travis's mouth. It was all she could do to keep from crying.

"He's in rare form this morning," Travis commented dryly, sipping at his coffee. "I hope he doesn't explode like that around the colts. They're high-spirited at the best of times."

"There's no need to worry. He isn't coming with us," Stacy said tightly, concentrating on the omelet on her plate.

"He's not?" A dark eyebrow flicked upward in a measuring look.

"No," she repeated.

"Did he give a reason?"

"Oh, yes," she nodded wryly. "He said he wasn't interested in a token involvement. He felt we were patronizing him by pretending he still made decisions about how the ranch was run."

"The entire breeding program for the quarter horses is his. Did you mention that?" Travis laughed without humor. "How are we supposed to know what he was trying to develop?"

"I don't think Cord cares anymore." There was a lump in her throat, large and painful. "He said we've run the ranch very capably without him and we can keep on doing it." Her eyes were clouded by inner distress as she glanced at the brawny man sitting opposite her. "He's convinced he isn't going to get any better."

"A man like Cord doesn't give up no matter what he says. Inside he keeps on fighting," Travis stated.

"Does he?" Stacy's chin quivered. "Today he said that he wished Colter hadn't pulled him out of the plane. I understand how he must feel, but—" she pressed a hand against her mouth to check the sob that rose in her throat "—he doesn't seem to care anymore about anything, not even the ranch." *Or me,* she could have added, but didn't.

"He denies that he cares because he cares too much."

"I wish I could believe that." Heaven knew that she tried. "It's my own fault that he feels the way he does about the ranch. Whenever there was a problem this past year, I wouldn't let you tell him about it until it was solved. I didn't want him worrying when it was so important that he rest. I let him think everything went smoothly. If I'd listened to you, Travis, Cord wouldn't think I was patronizing him now."

"Stacy, you can't tear yourself apart wondering if things would have been easier if you'd decided differently. What's done is done and we have to go on from here. Today we have a crop of yearlings to look at, so eat your breakfast." His voice was mockingly gruff but his smile was understandingly gentle.

Stacy returned the smile. "What you really mean is to get hold of myself." Her mouth curved in a self-deprecating line. "I don't know what I would have done if you hadn't been here to help this past year. And to listen."

"I hope I've been of use as a sounding board. You can't keep it bottled up inside without eventually breaking." He finished his coffee and set the mug on the table.

"What about you, Travis?" she probed softly, suddenly feeling guilty for burdening him with so many of her problems without a thought to his own hurt. "Have you needed a sounding board?"

Pain flickered briefly through his brown eyes. In his mind danced a haunting vision of a young woman with honey-brown hair and gold-flecked eyes—Natalie, the wife of his former boss, Colter Langston.

"Time." Travis breathed in deeply, chasing away the image. "Time has a way of healing things. Time and work."

Stacy left it at that, finishing the last mouthful of omelet.

"I want to speak to Cord before we get started with the work," she said.

"I'll come along if you don't mind." He rose from the chair, picking up his stained Western hat. "Maybe I can persuade him to come along with us."

Nodding agreement, she stepped away from the table.

She was skeptical of his chances of success, but at this point there was no harm in trying.

The broken glass and plates had been swept up. There was a darkened spot on the cobblestones where the liquid, either coffee or juice, hadn't completely dried.

Cord was sitting silently in his wheelchair as Stacy and Travis walked through the veranda doors. His hooded look never wavered from the distant hills, but Stacy knew he was aware of their approach.

"We're on our way to the stables," she said quietly.

"So?" Cord's voice seemed to come from a deep, dark place inside, a sarcastic inflection laced with disdain.

It was impossible to say that she wanted to be certain he was all right, and that he didn't need anything before she left. Cord was plainly revealing his scorn for any display of concern from her. She glanced hesitantly at Travis, wishing she hadn't felt the need to come out to the veranda.

Travis, with his usual unselfish perception, bridged the taut silence. "Cord, I'm a cattle-man. You ask me about Herefords or Angus or Santa Gertrudis and I can discuss their merits with anyone. Ask me about a good cowhorse and I'd know about that. But breeding horses and bloodlines, that's not my field."

An aloof black gaze swept to Travis. High cheek-bones accented the leanness of Cord's features, intensifying the patrician arrogance stamped in each chiseled line.

"Then you'd better learn." Indifference to the problem chilled Cord's reply.

"Cord!" Stacy breathed his name, frown-ing her protest to his continued withdrawn at-titude.

But the raven-dark head had already turned away, terminating further discussion of the subject. "Take the dog with you when you leave," Cord dismissed them coldly.

Stacy's patience evaporated. "Cajun can stay here." Temper trembled on the soft edges of her voice. "After you've driven everyone else away, Cord, you might be grateful for the company of man's best friend."

The impassive profile dipped slightly toward the black and tan shepherd lying beside the right wheel of his chair.

"You may have a point, Stacy," Cord replied evenly with the same degree of detachment as before. Then his gaze slashed at her. "A dog never stays with someone out of pity."

Her lips parted to reiterate that she loved him, but the lack of faith Cord had in the depth of her love for him hurt.

"You have a one-track mind, haven't you?" she accused hoarsely. "I would never feel sorry for you, Cord. You're too filled with self-pity for there to be any room for mine."

Pivoting sharply, she walked stiffly from the veranda. Seconds later, Travis's long strides had him walking beside her to the stables. She cast him a sideways glance, temper giving way to chagrin.

"I don't suppose I should have said that," she sighed. "He's always been able to make me lose my temper."

"I don't know if you should have or not." The grooves around his strong mouth deepened. "But if Cord is going to dish it out, he might as well learn to take it."

That sounded all well and good. True, she had turned the other cheek for a long time, but it didn't make her feel better to retaliate in kind. All she knew was that she would feel miserable until she apologized. Cord needed understanding. She should have appealed to his reason, not fed his anger.

Hank was standing in front of the stables when they approached. His leathered face, browned by the sun, hadn't aged at all in the nearly five years that Stacy had known him. He raised a hand in greeting, a glint of respect in the bright eyes when they focused on her.

From the stud pens, a sorrel stallion whickered to her, tossing his flaxen mane and stretching his neck over the rails. When Stacy failed to walk to him, Diablo whirled away from the board fence in a display of temper.

CHAPTER TWO

STACY SLID the veranda doors open and stepped through. The setting sun was casting a golden hue on the whitewashed adobe walls of the house. The crimson flowers of a bougainvillea provided a brilliant contrast.

Colorful Mexican pots, suspended by decorative macrame hangings, were overflowing with thick green foliage.

The German shepherd's tail thumped the cobblestoned floor.

He rose lazily from his place by Cord's wheelchair to walk to his mistress, thrusting a wet nose against her hand in affectionate greeting.

Cord glanced over his shoulder, his gaze raking Stacy from head to toe. There was no admiration, no approval, not even interest in his look.

She could have been wearing sackcloth and ashes instead of the richly dark hostess gown in gold that did attractive things to the light tan of her skin and the highlights in her hair.

"I thought you were doing book work in the study," he commented.

Yet his meaning seemed to be that if he had thought Stacy was going to come to the veranda, he wouldn't have been there.

"Not tonight." She moved nervously to one of the arched columns supporting the veranda roof. She thought she felt him watching her and turned, but Cord was studying the ripples of gold sunlight in the swimming pool.

"Paperwork has a way of piling up if not routinely handled," he said, then shrugged a shoulder. "But that's your affair."

His hands gripped the wheels of his chair, expertly spinning it around with a minimum of effort.

It was a full second before Stacy realized he was intending to reenter the house and leave her alone on the veranda.

"Cord, don't leave." She took a step toward him, then hesitated.

He stopped, turning his chair at an angle that would bring her into view.

The gold light of sunset bathed his features, changing them into a mask of pale bronze.

A dark eyebrow arched in arrogant question. "Why?"

"I want to talk to you."

Her voice broke slightly, driven to desperation by the way he had continually avoided her during the past two days.

"About what?"

His impassive expression didn't change. Not even an eyelash flickered.

"The things I said the other day—" nervously Stacy ran her fingers through her hair "—about your feeling sorry for yourself. I shouldn't have said that. I'm sorry."

The desire to rush to him was strong. She wanted to sit at his feet and rest her head on his lap. She wanted to feel his hand caressing her hair. If he had smiled even faintly, she would have. But the bronze mask didn't crack and pride kept her standing near the pillar.

"Does that mean you've reconsidered and decided that I don't feel sorry for myself?" His mouth twisted sardonically. "Or that you're sorry you said it?"

Her chin lifted a fraction of an inch. "To be truthful, Cord, I don't know how you think or feel anymore. You've started shutting me out. Every time I try to get close to you, some invisible barrier goes up and I'm on the other

side. I don't know how to reach you anymore.''

"I'm not shutting you out," he replied
evenly.

"Then what's happening?" Stacy lifted her
hands palm upward in a beseeching gesture,
asking to understand.

"Maybe you haven't adjusted to the fact
that now you're married to a cripple. Things
can't be the same as they were before the accident.''

"Why not?" she protested.

"You can never bring back yesterday.''

When Cord wheeled his chair through the
veranda doors, Stacy didn't call him back. Her
heart cried silently for the man who had once
laughed and smiled and had swept her into his
arms at the slightest provocation. Somewhere
behind that barrier of bitterness that man still
existed, but first Stacy had to find the key to
unlock the barrier or else batter down the
walls.

She doubted if she possessed the strength for
the battering.

She didn't sleep well that night. She tossed
and turned alone in her bed, haunted by the
memories of the nights she had spent in Cord's
arms and praying for their return.

The fear that Cord might be right and he would never walk again kept reasserting itself. Maybe she should face the possibility, but she refused to give up hope.

When she finally drifted into an exhausted sleep, she was determined not to let Cord give up hope, either.

Late the next day, she was in the study catching up on the paperwork she had let go the night before, when a car door slammed in the driveway, followed by the slamming of another door and the sound of young voices.

A quick smile lighted her face. The entry was never made in the ledger, as she rose from the desk and hurried into the foyer to the front door. She opened it at the same instant that a small black-haired boy with snapping dark eyes raced toward it.

"Mom!" he cried excitedly.

Her hands reached out, lifting him into her arms. "I've missed you, Josh!" she declared, kissing his tanned cheek and hugging him tightly.

He squirmed uncomfortably. He had informed her a month ago that he was getting too old for that mushy stuff, but habits die hard in mothers and Stacy was no exception.

However, with Jeff and Douglas Buchanan only a few steps behind Josh, she let him slide to the ground before she embarrassed him too severely.

"Did you have a good time?" she asked.

"You bet!" he nodded vigorously.

A string of details followed, ranging from Jeff riding him on the handlebars of his bicycle to the collection of rocks he had found. When he took time out for a breath, Stacy was certain he had only scratched the surface.

"Hold it!"

She held up a hand to stop the flow of words. "It sounds as if you could talk all night. But first I think you'd better help Mary bring your things to the house, don't you?"

Josh's dark eyes grew all round and innocent. "Bill is helping her, and he can carry a lot more than I can 'cause he's bigger than me."

"I bet there's something that is just your size you can carry," she said with a smile.

Stacy didn't doubt for an instant that those big dark eyes of her son had charmed his way out of a lot of things he hadn't wanted to do.

She took him by the shoulders and turned him back toward the big station wagon parked in the driveway.

"Go on."

She gave him a little shove toward the car and he moved reluctantly toward it.

A slight frown drew her brows together as Stacy glanced at the stocky man unloading Josh's tricycle. In order for Bill Buchanan to be free at this hour of the afternoon, he had to be combining a medical visit with a social call.

A quick mental calculation confirmed that Cord was just about due for another examination. A twinge of unease darted through her.

Her attention shifted to the red-haired woman walking toward her, Josh's small suitcase in her hand. "Hello, Mary," Stacy greeted. "You seem to have survived a week of Josh with no scars."

"With my two wild Indians, what's one more?" her friend laughed.

"He wasn't any trouble, was he?"

"None at all," Mary Buchanan assured her.

"I've got my rocks!" Josh came rushing toward the house again. This time he was proudly carrying a paper sack that bulged at the sides. "Where's daddy? I want to show him."

"I'm not sure. He's in the house somewhere," Stacy told him, and stepped to one side as Josh darted past without slowing up.

The two older boys followed at a more sedate pace.

"How are you, Stacy?" Bill Buchanan joined his wife.

"Fine, just fine," she answered quickly, perhaps too quickly.

A decidedly clinical eye scanned her features.

"I would say the circles under your eyes have got a bit darker," the doctor observed. "Part of the plan to have Josh spend a week with us was for you to get some rest. You can't keep burning the candle at both ends."

"I meant to rest," Stacy laughed, but it sounded brittle and artificial. "But I keep trying to catch up with all the work. It seemed that the more I did, the more there was to do."

"It's always that way," Mary agreed.

Stacy ignored the look of professional concern in Bill's eyes. Her problem was more than overwork. Somehow she couldn't bring herself to confide the truth.

Her relationship with Cord was strained— Travis knew because he saw them together so often.

"Come in and have something to drink. I don't know where my manners went." Quickly she changed the subject. "I'm certain Maria has some tea or lemonade in the refrigerator. Unless you would rather have coffee?''

"Something cold, I think," Mary responded, walking into the house. "What about you, Bill?"

"Yes, a cold drink will be fine. Where's Cord?" He glanced around the living room. "While you're rustling up some refreshments, I might as well see him. How's he doing, by the way, Stacy?"

"The same," she answered noncommittally. "If the boys are with him, by the sound of their voices, he's on the veranda."

"Probably buried beneath the pile of Josh's rocks," Mary laughed softly. "Whoever said little boys were made of snails and puppy-dog tails forgot to include rocks!"

"And toads and lizards and worms," Stacy added. "You two go ahead. I'll go to the kitchen and let Maria know you're here."

"I'll be on the veranda with the boys," Mary replied.

A few minutes later Stacy carried a tray of lemonade and cookies to the veranda. Neither Cord nor Bill was there.

It was several minutes before the three boys were situated with their glasses and cookies.

Stacy sank on to a chaise longue near Mary's chair.

"From the looks of you, I should have kept Josh another week," the redhead commented. "Bill is genuinely concerned about you, you know," she added gently.

"If you had kept Josh another week, I would have started worrying about him," Stacy smiled, trying to make light of Mary's remark.

"Seriously—" Mary shook her head "—how long do you think you can keep up this pace? You're trying to run the ranch, your home, take care of Josh, be a practical nurse for Cord and probably a hundred other things I haven't mentioned."

"I have a lot of help," Stacy pointed out. "If I didn't have Maria and Travis, I would have collapsed a long time ago. But it really isn't so bad, just hectic."

"Well, you should take a break and get away—for a little while if nothing else," Mary concluded.

"Cord needs me." A bittersweet smile played with the corners of Stacy's mouth. "If it was Bill, would you leave him?" She paused. "Even if it was for a little while?"

"No." There was a rueful grimace as Stacy made her point. "They would have to come and drag me away by force."

"Who would drag you where?" Bill pushed Cord's wheelchair through the opened veranda doors.

A warning glance from Stacy checked Mary's initial reply.

"If you didn't hear the first part of our conversation then I'm not going to tell you." The redhead switched her attention to the impassive man in the wheelchair. "Now that my husband is finished poking and pricking you all over, would you like something cold?"

"Yes, I would," Cord smiled, but Stacy noticed the brooding darkness in his eyes.

"I'll get it," she offered quickly when his gaze swung to her, piercing and searching.

"I'll do it," Mary insisted as Stacy started to rise from her chaise longue. "There's no need to stand on ceremony with us. Sit down and relax—heaven knows you have little enough opportunity to do that."

"Okay," Stacy submitted, and leaned back.

When Cord asked in low mockery, "Feeling overworked?" she wished she hadn't submitted so easily.

"Who doesn't?" she shrugged, ignoring the vague taunt.

"In one way or another, the spouses generally go through as much as the patients do," Bill commented almost absently.

Stacy tensed. Was it an idle remark, or had Bill caught the stinging inflection in Cord's voice? She glanced warily at Cord. A muscle twitching along the bronze jaw.

He was upset about something; she knew him too well not to recognize the signs.

A glass of iced lemonade was held out to him. Cord stared at it for several seconds before taking it and setting it on a wrought-iron stand near his chair. He impatiently waved aside the plate of cookies and let his gaze slice to Bill.

"How much longer is it going to be before someone finally admits that I'm not going to walk again?" he challenged.

Bill's blue eyes narrowed thoughtfully in the crushing silence that followed. "That depends," he said finally.

"On what?"

Cord tipped his head back, aggressively thrusting his chin forward.

"On whether you've decided that you can't walk," was the calm reply. "Miracles are in short supply, like everything else. A doctor can't snap his fingers and have you on your feet. It takes a combined effort of doctor and patient, with a bit of grace from God thrown in.''

"Which doesn't answer my question." One corner of the hard mouth quirked cynically, as if he expected the question to be dodged.

"Clinically speaking, the odds are still there that you will walk, but it isn't going to happen overnight."

A sound, something between laughter and contempt, rolled from Cord's throat. "That's a relief! For a minute there, I thought you were going to tell me this paralysis was psychosomatic."

"If I believed that," Bill said briskly, "I would have suggested a psychiatrist, not a—"

"Of course," Cord broke in sharply. His hands gripped the wheels, knuckles turning white under the strain of his hold. "Excuse me."

Before any of the three could speak, he was rolling his chair into the house.

The rigidity left Stacy in an uncontrollable shudder at his bitter display.

Bill's gaze swerved to her with professional sharpness.

"How long has this been going on?"

"Since shortly after he came home from the hospital this last time, almost constantly this last month," Stacy admitted.

Her eyes smarted with tears as she stared toward the house where Cord had gone.

"This ordeal would be rough on any man. As self-sufficient and independent as Cord has always been, I should have realized it would be even more difficult for him," the doctor murmured grimly.

Swallowing, she glanced nervously at him. "You suggested something to Cord. An operation?" She wasn't certain she could go through the anxiety of another operation and convalescence.

"No, I suggested a physiotherapist," he replied. "The simple exercises he's been doing have probably taken him as far as he can go on his own."

"What was Cord's reaction?"

She held her breath.

"Shall we say less than enthusiastic," Bill answered dryly.

"I'd like to shake him until his teeth rattled!" Mary declared. "Either way I don't envy the person who has to work with him. He can have a scorching tongue when he wants to cut somebody down to size."

"That's why I'm arranging to have Paula come." A faint smile of agreement with his wife's opinion curved his mouth. "She's the best I know."

"Paula? Paula Hanson?" Mary was suddenly alert. With an approving toss of her Titian hair, she turned to Stacy. "You'll like her."

"The question is—will Cord?" Stacy sighed.

"I doubt it," Bill chuckled. "But don't worry, Paula will be able to handle him. That girl not only knows her job, she also has an uncanny knack for knowing what tactics to use on her patient."

"She isn't exactly a girl, Bill," Mary corrected teasingly. "I think twenty-eight would qualify her as a woman."

"Is she married?"

Stacy glanced curiously at the two.

"So far, only to her career. She specializes in strictly the difficult cases, which is why I want her," Bill explained. "Paula once told me that by the time she gets acquainted with a new locale, it's time to move on to another case.

You can tell that she finds her work very re-warding.''

"Will she be living here—with us?" For some reason, Stacy found that thought unset-tling. She couldn't say exactly why.

A frown creased Bill's forehead as if he had considered the answer a foregone conclusion. "It would be easiest, if it wouldn't be too much trouble for you."

"I'm sure it wouldn't," she hastened. "I was only wondering what arrangements you'd been making."

"I'm sorry, I feel as though I've stuck my foot in my mouth," Bill apologized. "I should have consulted with you first before telling Paula that she could stay here. It wasn't very considerate of me."

"I'm in favor of anything or any arrange-ment that helps Cord," Stacy assured him.

"I suppose I was so delighted when she called me this morning to say she was released from the case she was on and would be avail-able to come here after a few days of rest that I never gave a thought to calling you first to clear things," he said ruefully.

"Bill, it really doesn't bother me. She's more than welcome to stay here." Yet there was an uncomfortable twinge of doubt. "I'm sure we'll get along."

"Don't judge her too quickly," he warned her. "Sometimes she comes on a little tough and blunt. But, if the saying was ever true that someone has a heart of pure gold, it fits Paula. She'll take some of the load of caring for Cord off your shoulders."

"Of course," Stacy smiled.

Inwardly she realized she was suffering from the pangs of jealousy. It was foolish and selfish to resent a woman she hadn't even met because she would be doing all the little things for Cord that Stacy was doing now.

It was difficult to get close to him. Paula Hanson's arrival would deny Stacy the few chances she had for closeness.

Recognizing the reason for her resentment also enabled Stacy to remember why Paula was coming. She was willing to sacrifice those moments with Cord if it would make him well again.

Mary and Bill Buchanan stayed for another hour. The conversation shifted from Cord to Josh and his visit with them.

Cord didn't return. When Stacy walked with the Buchanans to the front door, she noticed the door to his bedroom was closed.

He was still in there when Maria announced that dinner was ready. Stacy knew that if she went to the door he would simply say he wasn't hungry, so instead she sent Josh.

Cord wouldn't refuse his son.

The ploy worked as the three of them sat at the table together. Josh's nonstop chatter couldn't cover the brooding silence of his father, although Stacy was the only one to notice it.

"We played baseball, too," Josh declared, intent on relating everything he had done while he was gone. "Bill says I can hit pretty good. One time I hit a ball clear across the yard. That's a long way, huh?"

"It sure is," Stacy agreed, hiding a smile.

"Will you play ball with me tomorrow, dad?" Bright dark eyes were directed expectantly at his father. "And I'll show you the way I hit that ball."

Cord kept his dark gaze riveted to his plate, paling slightly beneath his tan. "It's difficult to play ball from a wheelchair, Josh," he responded with remarkable calm.

"I have an idea," Stacy spoke up quickly, trying to divert the sudden frowning look Josh was giving his father. "Why don't you and I play ball tomorrow? Daddy can watch while you show him how well you can hit the ball.''

"I guess so," Josh agreed. He pushed the peas around on his plate for several silent seconds, and then he frowned again at Cord and tipped his head to the side. "Dad, don't you get tired of watching all the time?"

Cord's fork clattered to the plate at Josh's question and Stacy rushed to answer. "Of course he does, but it can't be helped." Trying to distract him, she said, "Eat your dinner."

"I'm full." The small shoulders shrugged indifferently. He set his napkin on the table and leaned back in his chair, swinging his legs in rhythmic motion. "How much longer is it going to be before daddy gets better?"

Casting a sideways glance at Cord's grimly silent expression, she dodged the question.

"Long enough to make you ask questions. If you're through eating, you may be excused from the table. Ask Maria if she'll fix you an ice-cream cone to eat on the veranda."

Josh slid from his chair and walked unenthusiastically toward the kitchen. He left the room charged with tension. Stacy stared at her plate for several seconds. Pushing thick chestnut hair behind an ear, she looked at Cord.

"He's just a little boy. He doesn't understand about these things," she offered nervously, not knowing how to ease the pain her son's innocent remarks had caused.

"Doesn't he?" His gaze pinned her, arrogant and aloof. "I thought Josh put it very succinctly. I am bored and tired of watching all the time." Cord crumpled his napkin and tossed it onto the table. "Excuse me."

"Cord, the therapist who's coming—" Stacy began as he pushed himself away from the table.

But he interrupted her attempt to restore hope. "I don't want to talk about it" was his caustic reply.

CHAPTER THREE

STACY LIFTED her head from the pillow and listened. She was certain she had heard something. She waited. Had it been Josh crying out for her? There wasn't a sound in the quiet house.

She glanced at the luminous dial of her clock. One in the morning.

Nibbling at her lower lip, she waited a few more seconds, then with a sigh, she slipped out of bed. It was no use.

She wouldn't go back to sleep until she had made certain Josh was all right.

It was crazy, but all the while he had been staying at the Buchanans', she hadn't woken once during the night to check on him. Yet this was only his first night at home and she was already instinctively listening for him.

Her peach-colored robe was lying near the foot of the bed. Throwing it around her shoulders, Stacy walked barefoot to the hall door. Silence greeted her as she entered the corridor. She relied on her memory to make her way in the darkness to Josh's room across the hall from hers.

She opened the door quickly, stepping in to see him sleeping peacefully beneath the red and blue covers of his spread. Moonlight streamed in from the window, touching his black hair and magically lacing it with silver.

As she started to close the door, she heard what sounded like a low moan. Was it the wind rubbing a branch outdoors, she wondered. But there wasn't a strong wind, only the gentlest of breezes.

Then it came again. From downstairs, Stacy thought. Was it Cord? Her heart skipped a beat in fear that he might have fallen and was unable to pull himself up.

Her feet barely touched the steps as she raced down the unlit staircase to the master bedroom she had shared with Cord until the accident. A low, deep moan sounded on the other side of the door and she flung it open.

A small night-light illuminated his long shape in the bed. It glistened over the golden tan of his complexion. The black of his hair contrasted sharply with the white pillowcase.

His head rolled to one side. A tortured sound came from his throat, escaping his lips in the low moan that Stacy had heard. Swiftly she moved to his side, pausing for a frightened second when she saw the perspiration beading his face. Again his head moved restlessly to the side.

Stacy realized with relief that he wasn't ill or fevered. He was dreaming, it was a nightmare. Lightly she laid a hand on his shoulder.

"Cord, wake up," she whispered softly. "You're dreaming. Everything is all right. It's just a dream. Wake up!"

His face twisted as if in pain. He shook his his head as though trying to chase away the image that frightened him. Her hands tightened on his shoulder.

"Cord, wake up," she repeated.

Sooty lashes raised as Cord stared at her blankly. His fingers closed over the wrist of her hand resting on his shoulder. She could feel him trying to fight through the misty waves that still gripped his consciousness.

"Josh?" he frowned harshly. "Is he all right?"

"He's fine," she nodded, smiling to reassure him.

"Are you sure?" Cord lifted his head from the pillow.

"I'm positive," Stacy said. "I just looked in on him before I came downstairs. He's sound asleep."

Cord sank back against the pillow, breathing shakily. "My God!" he shuddered. "I had this nightmare."

His fingers were biting so tightly into her wrist that he was nearly cutting off the circulation. Stacy leaned against the bed, half sitting on the edge. With her free hand, she took a tissue from the bedside table and began wiping the perspiration from his forehead.

"It was only a dream," she repeated.

Cord sighed heavily. "He was in the swimming pool and he couldn't swim."

"You know that Josh swims like a fish," she chided him gently.

"I know, but this time he couldn't. I don't know why." Cord shook his head wearily and gazed into a dark corner of the room. "He kept crying for me to stop watching and save him. But I couldn't move. I—"

"Sssh!" She touched a fingertip to his lips and he turned to look at her. His dark eyes mirrored the tormenting anguish that consumed him. "Forget about the dream."

Cord loosened the grip on her wrist without releasing it.

With his other hand, he stilled the wiping motion of her free hand, making it rest along the hard line of his jaw.

Sighing heavily, he seemed to banish the last remnant of the nightmare.

As if he needed her nearness to keep it from coming back, he slowly slid his arms around her and pulled her down to his chest. Her head was nestled near the hollow of his throat.

"It was so real," he murmured, wrapping his arms around Stacy to hold her there.

"I know." There was a slight catch in her voice.

Beneath her hand, she could feel the uneven thud of his heart. The cloud of dark, curling hair on his chest tickled her cheek. Her arm was curved across his chest, her hand resting on the silken hardness of his shoulder.

The heady male scent of him was heightened by the perspiration that had flowed through his pores at the peak of his nightmare. It filled her senses with sensual intoxication.

Her heart skipped several beats at the caressing warmth of his breath stirring her hair. Almost of its own volition, her hand began lightly exploring the smooth muscles of his shoulder and the strong column of his neck.

A large, well-shaped hand moved down her spine, drawing her closer to him. Then lazily it began rubbing the curve of her waist. A searing contentment swept through her and Stacy sighed. There was no barrier between them now.

Cord pressed his mouth against the side of her hair for an instant, then rubbed the roughness of his cheek against the silken strands.

"Sometimes," he murmured huskily, "I lie awake nights remembering how it was when you lay all soft and warm beside me."

He slid a hand beneath her thick chestnut hair, curling it gently on the side of her neck. His thumb moved in a rhythmic circle on the sensitive cord. Shivers of joy danced over her skin as her heart quickened its pace.

"I remember the clean fragrance of your hair." Cord nuzzled the side of her head. "And the way you trembled when I touched you, your breasts swelling hard in my hand. I can still see the golden glow of your warm skin when you lay naked beside me, waiting, your eyes shimmering like brown silk with the fire we'd kindled."

Stacy was trembling, the same liquid fire racing again through her veins. The seductive pitch of his voice was arousing more than just a memory. Her head was tipped back over the curve of his arm. Her lashes closed as Cord softly brushed his lips over her eyes, teasing the corners and kissing the gold dust of freckles over the bridge of her nose.

"And your lips." He tantalized their quivering moistness. "The taste of your mouth, like a honeyed nectar that drugs the senses and never satisfies the thirst. I would drink and drink and drink and come back for more."

A soft moan of aching desire rolled over her tongue, his words teasing and stimulating her until she thought her reeling mind would never be sober again. She felt the crook of his smile against her skin.

"Most of all I remember the catlike sounds you made in your throat. What I don't remember—" there was an amused tone of gentle mockery in his low voice as he slid a hand to the neckline of her robe "—is you wearing so much to bed."

"That's because it wasn't on long enough for you to notice," Stacy murmured with a sighing laugh.

Her fingers wound themselves into the raven thickness of his hair. With the slightest pressure, she ended the exquisite torture of his teasing mouth. Her heart rocketed under the commanding hardness of his kiss.

His mouth opened over hers, tasting the sweetness of her lips before parting them to familiarly explore her mouth. Deftly Cord untied her robe and cast it to the floor.

The narrow strap of her nightgown left her smooth shoulders bare to his caress.

The passionate embrace was a catalyst that released all the pent-up longings they had held in check for so long. The intimate touch of his hands made her feel more alive than she had in ages.

The days, the months, the strain of being together yet apart fled on silver wings as Stacy gave herself up to the joy of the moment that transcended a mere physical response.

Twisting a handful of hair, Cord tipped her head farther back to expose her throat to the bruising ardor of his mouth.

Stacy shuddered as he moved inexorably closer to the shadowy cleft between her breasts and arched toward him. Her fingers dug deep into the hard flesh of his arms.

In the next second, Cord was pushing her away from him with a groan.

A bare foot touched the cool tile of the floor to keep her balance. Still quivering from his lovemaking, she gazed at him numbly, her eyes luminous and very soft.

"I love you, Cord."

Her voice trembled.

His breathing was labored, and Stacy knew he was shaken as she was. In the dim light, she could see the frown creasing his wide forehead.

His eyes were tightly closed as if trying to shut out the sight of her.

With a nearly inaudible moan she glided back to the broad chest, sliding her arms around his shoulders to cling to him.

But his hands closed punishingly over the soft flesh of her upper arms and shoved her away.

"Stacy, don't," Cord demanded in a tormented groan.

Her fingers trailed over the rigid muscles in his arms as they held her away. She made them take her weight in an effort to lessen the distance between them.

"I want you to hold me," she protested in an aching murmur. "Just hold me for a little while. It's been so long since I've had your arms around me or known your kisses."

"And what about the agony of an unful-filled embrace?" he taunted in half-anger. "Don't torment us with that."

"You're wrong, darling," Stacy cried softly. "I can be satisfied with kisses. It's better than going without touching you or feeling you caress me."

"I know you better than that," Cord breathed. "We've spent too many nights together for me to forget that core of passion inside you. A touch—a kiss—isn't enough for either of us, not ultimately."

His words chilled her.

"What are you saying?" She frowned warily, almost afraid to hear his answer.

"That I don't accept crumbs," He answered crisply. "I would always be tasting the whole loaf and wanting it."

Stiffening, Stacy pulled away from his iron grip. "What about what I want? What I need?"

"Dammit, Stacy," he swore softly in frustration. His jaw was clenched, the line of his mouth grimly forbidding. "I can't come to you half a man."

Her chin quivered as she straightened away from the bed. "So you won't come to me at all, is that it?" she accused tightly. "And I'm not supposed to touch you or kiss you no matter how much I want to, is that what you're saying?"

"What I'm saying," Cord snapped, "is that if you go without food long enough, you stop being hungry."

"Do you, Cord?" flashed Stacy. Her heart was nearly bursting with pain. "Or do you just die?"

A muscle leaped in his jaw. "Not entirely." He scowled and looked away from her, his gaze again seeking the dark recesses of the room. "Although I've wished for it." He rubbed a numb thigh with his hand. "I have learned how a wild animal feels when he's caught in a trap and can't escape."

"But you aren't going to be trapped forever," she retorted. "You will walk again. Why can't you accept that? Why can't you believe that?"

"And why can't you accept the possibility that I may never walk again?" Cord growled.

"If I did, then what? Do you expect us to go on the rest of our lives with you sleeping in one room and me in the other? Never touching? Never kissing? Never showing our love for each other?" she challenged.

"I expect you to understand," he snapped impatiently. "My God, don't you know what it's like? Don't you know what it is remembering what we once shared? Then you ask me to love with virtually half of my body dead. I would prefer endless nightmares to that."

"It isn't dead," Stacy protested angrily.

The faint glow from the night-light glistened over the golden tan of his naked physique. Always leanly muscled, there was now a sinewy look about him, a result of the weight loss he had suffered.

Yet it didn't detract from his dark looks. He still possessed vitality, an aura of virility, a touch of aloof arrogance, a dozen other indefinable qualities that singled him out as something special.

One corner of his mouth lifted in a cynical sneer. "Are you denying that I can't use my legs?"

"You can't use them now, no, but—" she brushed the hair away from her face, helplessly searching for the words to put forth her argument "—that doesn't mean it will always be that way."

"And it doesn't mean that it won't," he countered.

"The therapist Bill is sending here—he wouldn't have her come if he didn't think she could help you. Don't you realize that?" Stacy pleaded in a desperate kind of anger.

Cord breathed in deeply, a brooding look in his dark eyes.

"Sometimes I have the feeling that I'm a human guinea pig. Or a jigsaw puzzle that was put together in the wrong order and now the pieces don't fit so they're trying to force them."

The weary despair in his voice touched her. Stacy couldn't help flinching at the strong undercurrent of monotonous pain that made his tone sound dull and flat.

"You mustn't feel that way," she protested.

"Why?" A dark eyebrow lifted in dry amusement. "For nearly a year, I've listened to one person after another telling me how good my chances are that I'll walk again. I keep hearing it and hearing it, but I'm still either in a wheelchair or a bed. Hopeful words are wearing thin."

"Maybe the therapist will help," Stacy offered weakly.

"There goes another maybe," he laughed without humor. "Maybe the therapist. Maybe the operation," Cord mocked. "It will be another blind alley that the wheelchair will take me out of.''

"But what's the alternative?" she protested. "Not to try at all? Don't you want to walk?"

"That's not the point." His mouth thinned grimly.

"Forgive me, but I don't understand." Stacy walked to the end of the bed, her fingers gripping the bedrail until her knuckles were white. "What is the point?"

"I'm tired of constantly having hope build up like air in a balloon, then watching it slowly deflate when it comes to nothing. Not just my own, but yours and Josh's, everyone's. I don't want you to be hurt anymore because of me." Cord stared at her for a long moment, a silent ache in his eyes. "I've seen it happen and I've seen the way you try to hide it so I won't see. But I do."

Stacy shook her head. "Forget about what it's doing to Josh and me. Look what it's doing to you!" she argued. "You've become hard and embittered. I can't even come near you anymore. You don't want me to touch you or kiss you. You just keep retreating farther and farther away, living in your own little world. It must be terribly lonely there. Maybe you're tired of fighting, tired of trying and failing—I don't know.''

"You haven't listened to anything I've said,'' Cord declared irritably.

"I have,'' she nodded. "You're trying to tell me that the chances are you won't walk again. You want me to admit that. All right, I do.'' Anger was building inside her, an anger born because he persisted in looking at the negative side. "You're a cripple, Cord. A cripple! Do you hear?'' Suddenly Stacy wanted to hurt him with words as he had hurt her. "You'll always be a cripple! If that's the way you want to look at life, that's the way I'll look at it, too!''

Moisture was dampening her cheeks, and Stacy realized she was crying. Her vision had blurred to the point where she could only make out a dim shape of him.

She caught back a sob of pain and pivoted sharply around.

"Stacy!''

But she was flying from the room, sobs wracking her body with each racing, stumbling step. In her room, she threw herself onto the bed, drowning her pillow with tears.

She had held them back for nearly a year, but now the deluge had begun.

The ravages of the storm were visible in her face the next morning. Maria clucked anxiously around her, certain the swollen eyes, red nose and pale complexion were the symptoms of a cold. Stacy insisted she was fine, but her gaze kept straying to the closed door of the master bedroom.

Only Josh shared the breakfast meal with her. Cord remained in his room. On her way out of the house, she paused at the door, wanting to go in and apologize yet not knowing what to say. Finally she walked out to meet Travis.

There was so much that had to be done in preparation for the annual quarter-horse sale the ranch held. Stacy wished she had broken the tradition and postponed it.

She was a trembling mass of nerves, unable to concentrate. She kept remembering the first sale she had organized for Cord. It had been that day—the day of the auction—when she had been on the verge of leaving that he had told her he loved her and asked her to marry him.

Finally Travis had told her he would take care of the rest of the duties and suggested that she take the morning off. Stacy couldn't bring herself to go back to the house.

She didn't want to face Cord until she had control of herself.

If anyone looked at her crooked, she felt she would burst into tears.

Not once had she broken down when she had learned of Cord's plane crash, nor during her flight to his side, nor during the harrowing hours and days after surgery. When he had regained consciousness, Stacy had rejoiced with laughter and warmth. Now it had all caught up with her and it seemed she couldn't stop crying.

A tear slipped from her lashes. She wiped it away with a shaking hand. Releasing a sobbing sigh, she turned away from the house and walked toward the stables.

Hank ambled forward to meet her, his sharp eyes missing nothing.

"Hi, Hank." Stacy greeted the man with forced brightness. "Would you saddle my mare for me? I thought that I'd take a ride and chase away some of the tension."

"Sure will," he agreed.

Minutes later he led the chocolate-brown mare from the stable, saddled and bridled and ready to go. The breeze stirred the horse's flaxen mane as it nosed Stacy affectionately.

With Hank holding the bridle, she stepped into the saddle and gathered the reins in her hand. Hank remained at the horse's head, his wizened face inspecting her.

"The boss don't like for you to go out ridin' by yourself," he said quietly.

"I promise I won't go far."

Stacy smiled, but her voice broke at the end of her sentence.

There was only one person that Hank ever referred to as the boss, and that was Cord. She touched her heels to the mare's flanks and reined it away before Hank saw the shimmer of tears in her eyes. The sorrel stallion in the stud pen whickered forlornly as she rode away.

CHAPTER FOUR

A TEXAS spring was impossible to ignore. After leaving the ranch buildings, Stacy had given the mare her head.

They cantered through the meadow where the brood mares with new colts were pastured. Colorful blossoms of bluebonnets, Mexican hats and prickly poppies nodded and bowed their heads as Stacy and the mare went by.

Bees buzzed from blossom to blossom while bright butterflies lazily flitted along.

The creak of saddle leather and the dull thud of cantering hooves were soothing sounds to Stacy's jangled nerves.

To the west were the mountains, once the stronghold of the Mescaleros. A dusty haze obscured them.

Although raised in the city, Stacy was still a country girl. The land rejuvenated her, especially this land where she lived with Cord. It was her home and she loved it.

She could ride for hours over its vast reaches and never tire of it.

Sighing, she reined the mare in and turned her toward the ranch yard. Unfortunately she didn't have time for such indulgences. There were a hundred and one things to be done at the ranch today. Stacy decided she had better get them done while her eyes were dry and the pain in her chest had been reduced to a funny little ache.

Hank was waiting at the pasture gate to let her through.

She guessed he had been watching for her for some time, although it seemed she had barely left. His concern touched her.

"You see, I made it back all in one piece." Dimples appeared in her cheeks as she teased him affectionately.

"You shore took your time about comin' back," he declared with mock gruffness. He took hold of the mare's bridle and held her while Stacy dismounted. "I was about to send someone out to look for you when I saw you in the meadow."

"You're worse than a mother hen," she chided.

"Yeah, well, it'd be my back the boss would climb on if anything was to happen to you."

"What could happen riding Candy Bar?"

She handed the reins to him, patting the mare's neck.

"I was beginnin' to wonder that myself," Hank grumbled.

"Would you mind walking her out for me?" she asked.

At his agreeing nod, Stacy angled toward the ranch house sitting on a slight knoll above the other buildings. Josh was playing in the front yard. When he saw her coming, he hopped on his tricycle and rode down the graveled driveway to meet her, varooming all the way.

"Where have you been, mommy?" he asked as he wheeled along side of her.

"I went for a ride," she smiled into the darkly bright eyes.

Josh immediately scowled at her answer. "I wanted to go, too," he protested.

"Another time, maybe," she suggested.

"That's what you always say," he grumbled. "You'll forget, I know you will."

"How could I possibly forget you!" As they started up the knoll, Stacy slowed her steps as Josh's small legs pedaled harder to keep up.

"Will you play ball with me?" He glanced up at her quickly, the scowl leaving his face. His foot slipped off a pedal and he nearly rolled down the hill before Stacy could grab the handlebars. "You said you would," he reminded her.

"I can't now, Josh." She shook her chestnut hair in a rueful gesture. "I have work to do. Later, okay?"

"Promise?"

"I promise."

Stacy crossed her heart with her fingers and he was satisfied.

"I hit grounders best of anything," he told her importantly.

"I'll bet you do." She hid a smile and nodded. They had reached the sidewalk to the house. "You stay outside and play until lunchtime, okay? But don't go out of the yard."

"Okay, mom."

The level sidewalk offered a perfect straightaway and Josh was already careening down it as he shouted his answer.

A faint smile played on her lips as she opened the front door.

Walking in, she turned to close it, darting a tenderly maternal glance at her son.

"It's about time you got back!" a harshly censorious voice growled behind her.

Her shoulders stiffened under the piercing regard of Cord's gaze, then slowly she turned to meet it. Her barely healed nerves were suddenly fraying again, disintegrating from the sharp undercurrents slicing the air.

Cord's wheelchair blocked the foyer entrance into the living room. A clenched jaw made his lean features taut and forbidding. His narrowed black gaze pinned her.

Somehow she managed to close the door.

"Were you looking for me?" she inquired with forced calm.

"I wasn't looking for you," he informed her in a steely voice. "I was listening to everyone else tell me how ill you looked."

His gaze raked her mercilessly, nearly stripping away the thin veneer of composure that she had attained. Her mouth tightened, guessing that Maria was the talebearer and wishing the woman had kept silent.

"I hardly think it was everyone," she murmured, avoiding direct contact with his gaze.

"First Maria, then Travis, then Bill," Cord enumerated tersely.

"Bill?"

Stacy frowned at the name.

"The good doctor telephoned a little while ago to let you know that this Hanson woman will be arriving here on Friday.'' The sarcastic explanation was snapped out.

"How did he know about me?''

Immediately she wished that she hadn't worded the question that way.

It was an admission that she hadn't been herself when she had risen this morning. Despite her embittered statements last night, Stacy didn't want Cord becoming concerned about her.

Because right now he needed to concentrate on his own recovery.

"Maria answered the telephone,'' Cord explained. "By the time I talked to him, he was more worried about where you were.''

"I went for a ride.''

Stacy flipped her long chestnut hair away from her neck, striving for a nonchalance that she just didn't feel.

"Alone.''

The accusation was sharply hurled at her.

Her head jerked slightly. "Who told you?'' Surely Hank wouldn't have.

The strong, male line of his mouth tightened grimly. "I saw you leave the stables.'' With suppressed violence, he swung the wheelchair around toward the living room. "Dammit, Stacy, you already know how I feel about you wandering out on the range by yourself!''

Stacy flinched. "Yes, Hank reminded me," she said in a low voice.

He pushed the chair a few feet into the room and stopped.

"Suppose your mare had fallen or you'd been thrown. Do you want me to start having nightmares about you lying unconscious in some remote place? Is that why you did it?" he challenged tightly.

"No." Stacy followed him, her hands clasped nervously together. "I had to get away for a while, to be by myself and think."

"Alone on a horse?" he jeered. "I didn't realize that was a necessity for thinking."

"You don't understand. I had to get away," she began desperately.

"No, I don't understand!" Cord interrupted. "If you wanted to be alone, you could have just as easily gone to your room. There would have been considerably less danger than riding alone."

"I couldn't stay in the house. Everything closed in around me. I had to get away from—" She stopped abruptly, glancing at him.

A sardonic eyebrow shot up.

"From me?" Cord finished the sentence for her.

Stacy hesitated, then admitted, "Yes, from you. Last night—"

She wanted to say that she had said some things that she regretted, but her tongue tied itself in knots over the words.

"What about last night?"

His dark head was tilted to one side at a watchful angle.

She couldn't meet his alert gaze and turned her back to him. Her stomach was twisted into knots. There was a throbbing pain in her temples as her poise began to splinter.

"I can't take many more of these bitter arguments. I need to get away from this brittle atmosphere—"

A sob rose in her throat and she had to stop to swallow it. She didn't want to break down in front of Cord again.

"I thought that was what this was leading up to," Cord declared, exhaling harshly. "I should probably be surprised that it's taken you so long."

Stacy pivoted to look at him blankly. The disgust etched in his drawn features nearly took her breath away.

A smoldering fire darkened his eyes to the shade of hard black diamonds, just as sharp and cutting.

"There's no need to look so puzzled," he mocked with contemptuous sarcasm. "Bill has already paved the way for you. Did you cry on his shoulder last night?"

"I don't know what you're talking about." She frowned in genuine confusion.

"Don't you? Didn't you just say that you needed to get away?" he countered arrogantly.

"Yes, but—" Her shoulders moved bewilderedly.

"It was Bill's medical opinion, too, that you needed a few weeks' rest away from me and the ranch." Cord breathed in deeply, his chin thrust forth in challenge. "He seemed to think you were under too much stress. Your nerves were becoming strained, on the verge of collapse, he said."

Stacy opened her mouth, wanting to deny it, yet secretly she feared the same thing. At this moment, she was trembling badly and she couldn't make herself stop.

"It hasn't been easy for me," she murmured finally.

"Did you stage that outburst last night so I would be convinced when Bill talked to me today, knowing all the while that he would call?" Cord accused.

"No!" she gasped in wounded outrage.

"And you made certain this morning that others saw how upset you were," added Cord, totally ignoring her denial.

"You were the one who had the nightmare," Stacy reminded him indignantly. "You woke me—that's why I came to your room. And you were the one who started the entire argument with your stupid pride and self-pity, and your insistence that there mustn't be any physical contact between us. Did you expect me to just bow my head and say whatever you wish, my lord?" she flashed.

"Don't pretend with me, Stacy!" There was a savage note in the controlled anger of his reply. "I should have known that it wouldn't last. I should have guessed why you kept clinging so desperately to the vain hope that I might walk again. I have to give you credit for trying."

"Pretend? Trying? What are you talking about?" she demanded, now thoroughly confused. "Everything I've said is the truth. I didn't ask Bill to tell you I should have a few weeks' rest. When he suggested it to me, I told him no."

Cord laughed coldly.

"Whatever you do, don't destroy the image of a loving wife," he mocked bitterly. "Be sure to twist things around and make it look as if you're the injured party."

"I never claimed to be the injured party," Stacy cried helplessly.

"Others will do it for you."

The grooves around his mouth deepened with cynicism.

"Why?"

"Out of sympathy because you're married to a cripple, a man who's become short-tempered and embittered," Cord replied.

"At least you admit that," she muttered beneath her breath.

"Yes, I admit that," he said grimly. "Why won't you admit that what I'm saying is true?"

"But I don't know what you are saying." There was a frustrated ring to her protesting cry.

"You've finally become bored with ranch life, haven't you?" Cord studied her with freezing aloofness.

"What?" She was stunned.

"It wasn't so bad before the crash, was it?" he taunted. "We traveled around a great deal, a horse-buying trip or an odd weekend to shop. Josh kept you busy when he was a baby. And the ranch life was still a new experience for you at first. Then—" he reached down and gripped his leg, his mouth quirking "—the accident happened."

He lifted his gaze from the wheelchair to her. Stacy was so shocked by what he was implying that she couldn't speak.

She stared at him in disbelief.

"This past year, it's been different. You've been chained to either the ranch or the hospital," continued Cord. "Life has become tedious, with no side trips to break the monotony. You're bored. Being young, you want some excitement in your life. You want to see and do things, just have fun once in a while."

"My father took me all over the world with him," she protested, remembering her travels with him as a freelance photographer. "I've seen everything."

"Which makes it all the more understandable why you can't settle for the dull routine of a ranch, miles from any cosmopolitan center." For all the unemotional quality in his voice, the cold glare of his eyes was condemning. "You don't want to accept the possibility that I might be an invalid for the rest of my life because that would mean the boredom would never end. There wouldn't be any more quick trips, no vacations, no dancing, no fun. Just a lifetime of taking care of me."

"I don't mind," Stacy insisted.

"For how long?" he questioned arrogantly. "Right now you feel guilty about leaving me alone. That's why you've contrived this incident where someone else suggests that you go away for a rest. It wouldn't be your idea that way."

"I didn't do anything of the kind," she denied angrily, wondering how he could make such an accusation.

"Yes, you did, dammit. Now admit it," Cord snarled. "You think that if you leave me for a few weeks, it wouldn't be so bad when you come back. But in six months, you'll be bored again and want to leave for another 'short' respite. A couple of months after you come back from that, you'll want to go again until finally you won't want to come back at all."

"That's not true. This is my home!" Her temper flared at the continued injustice of his remarks. "You don't know what you're talking about!"

"Yes, I do!" He was virtually shouting now, his voice rolling like thunder over her. "You're forgetting my mother! She was accustomed to the luxuries of life the same as you were. She was pampered and spoiled. At first the roughness, the earthiness of ranch life appealed to the adventurous side of her nature, too, but she soon tired of it, and eventually she went back to the so-called civilized world!"

"I'm not like your mother was!"

Stacy denied it vehemently, her brown eyes flashing.

"Aren't you?" he jeered. "I'll bet you didn't even intend to take Josh with you when you went on Bill's medically recommended vacation. You would leave him the same way my mother left me."

"I would not leave him! And I'm not going on any vacation!" she cried.

"You're damned right you're not!" Cord agreed savagely. "Because I'm not my father! I won't let you go. You're staying right here with me."

"I'm staying here of my own free will!" Stacy declared. "Not because you order me or command me to stay!"

His hands gripped the arms of his wheel-chair, the muscles rippling in his forearms at the strangling hold. It was difficult to believe he wasn't able to get out of the chair and have those long strides of his carrying him to her side.

"You will stay here and be my wife." He gave no indication that he had heard what she said. "You will abide by the vows we made to each other. In sickness and in health."

"One of them we said wrong." Her voice was starting to break, an uncontrollable anger trembling on the edges. "It should have been for *bitter* or worse!"

Pivoting, Stacy would have run from the room. A small, dark-haired boy stood in the opening to the veranda.

His rounded eyes were black pools of agony as he gazed from the glowering face of his father to Stacy's whitened features.

The crushing silence lasted only a few seconds, but they were tortuous ones as both Stacy and Cord realized Josh had overheard their heated argument. Stacy recovered her wits first, taking a sharp step toward him.

Josh immediately started to retreat, half turning as if to run.

"Joshua!" Cord's commanding voice checked his flight. He darted a frightened look at his father. When Cord spoke again, the bite of anger was out of his voice. "Come here, Josh. It's all right." Although said calmly, it was no less imperative.

Josh hesitated, glancing at Stacy. "It's all right." She added her reassurance to Cord's and held out her hand to her son.

With obvious reluctance, he walked toward her, his feet dragging. The silken black head was tilted downward, but his troubled dark eyes warily watched both his parents, peering at them through thick curling lashes.

There was a scalding ache in Stacy's heart when he stopped cautiously in front of her, ignoring her outstretched hand.

Kneeling, she placed her trembling hands on his small shoulders. They were stiff and silently resistant to her touch.

"It's okay, Josh," she reassured him again in a shaky voice. "We were arguing, that's all. You've heard mommy and daddy quarrel before."

"You were yelling at each other," he accused, his lower lip jutting out slightly.

He could tell that this time it was different, more than a mere disagreement.

Nibbling at her lower lip, she glanced at Cord. His expression was grim, his mouth clamped shut in a tight line.

He had clasped his hands in his lap. They gripped each other with punishing fierceness.

"Y—your daddy was upset with me," Stacy began, trying to give him an explanation he would understand.

It was difficult. The emotionally charged scene with Cord was still whirling in her mind.

The thousand tiny knife cuts inflicted by his words dulled her thinking.

"Why?" Josh prompted in an unconvinced tone.

"Because—I'd gone riding by myself." She smiled tightly, running a hand over the sleeve of his shirt, wanting to draw the little boy into her arms. "You see, daddy became upset because I might have fallen and got hurt. Since I was all by myself, no one would know. And sometimes, when you're very upset because you care about someone, you start yelling."

Josh looked at Cord out of the corner of his eye, seeking confirmation of her explanation. Cord breathed in deeply, relaxing the death grip of his hands.

"That's true, Josh," he agreed.

Turning back to Stacy, Josh inspected the brittle calm of her expression. A niggling uncertainty remained in his dark eyes.

"Are you going away, mommy?"

"Of course not." She quickly busied her hands, straightened the collar of his shirt. "Why, if I went away, who would tie your shoes?" she teased wanly.

"Daddy said you were," Josh reminded her.

"Daddy said—" she swallowed the lump in her throat "—that I was going to stay here with you and him forever and ever and ever. Because we're a family."

"Are you sure?" he blinked.

"I'm sure," Stacy nodded.

"Okay," Josh grinned in satisfaction.

"Say, I have an idea." She brushed a forefinger across the tip of his nose in play.

"What's that?" his eyes were bright and clear as he cocked his head to the side curiously.

"Instead of waiting until this afternoon, why don't we play ball now?" she suggested.

"Yeah!" he breathed excitedly. "And daddy can come outside with us, too, huh?"

"Ask him," Stacy smiled stiffly.

There was a time when she could have answered for Cord. But after the things he had said to her, he seemed practically like a stranger. She didn't seem to know him at all.

Josh turned eagerly to Cord. "Will you come to watch us, dad?"

"Yes," he agreed with a curt nod.

Straightening, Stacy ruffled the silky soft hair on top of her son's head.

"Go and find your bat and ball," she said. "We'll meet you outside in a few minutes."

Not needing a second invitation, Josh was off with a rush. Stacy's gaze followed him, watching the doorway for several seconds after he had disappeared from view. Wearily she slid her fingers through her hair, lifting it away from her face, and turned to walk toward Cord.

She felt drained.

"I'll help you outside," she muttered, heading toward the back of his wheelchair.

As she drew alongside of him, his hand closed over her wrist to halt her. She glanced down, stoically meeting his hooded look.

"I owe you an apology," Cord said quietly. A new life started to flow in her veins, only to be aborted by his next statement. "You could have easily used Josh as a weapon against me, but you didn't."

Stacy twisted her wrist away from his hand. "That's a hateful thing to say," she accused in a choked voice. "He is *our* son, not mine or yours. I would never make him take sides."

"I did apologize for thinking it," he reminded her tautly.

"Lately I don't know you." She stared at him almost fearfully. "I feel as if I'm living with a stranger. I don't see how you can imagine for one minute that I feel about you or our home the way your mother did."

Cord studied her silently, his lips twisting cynically. "But you were the one who told me yourself that you couldn't take much more and that you needed to get away. I didn't imagine that."

"But—" The beginnings of another argument formed on her tongue. Stacy paused and shook her head hopelessly. "Don't let's start this all over again."

"We won't," he stated. "I only want to remind you that you're my wife and I'm never letting you go."

Stacy bridled at the ring of possession in his voice. It was the same tone that had once thrilled her when it was spoken with love instead of ruthless determination. So much had changed.

"We'd better go outside." She stifled the urge to make a cutting retort and stepped behind his wheelchair. "Josh will be waiting for us." She pushed him toward the opened veranda doors.

CHAPTER FIVE

"MARIA." STACY stepped into the kitchen, adjusting the wide-brimmed hat on her head.

"Si." The plump Mexican woman was standing in front of the sink, washing the breakfast dishes. She glanced over a shoulder at Stacy without pausing in her work.

"I'm leaving now with Travis to check on the cattle the boys are moving to the summer range," she told the housekeeper. "I should be back shortly before lunch if anyone calls. Josh is playing out front."

"I will keep an eye on him," the older woman promised.

"Thanks, Maria." Stacy turned to leave, then pivoted back.

"Oh—Miss Hanson, the woman Dr. Buchanan has hired to help Cord, should be arriving sometime today. If she comes while I'm gone, you can put her things in the room down the hall from mine."

"I have it all aired and cleaned for her," Maria assured her.

"Good. I'll see you later." Stacy waved briefly and hurried down the hallway to the front door.

As she passed Cord's room, she heard the radio playing, but she didn't stop to tell him she was leaving. If he wondered where she was, he could ask Maria.

The barrier between them was as solid and as cold as a polar ice cap. There wasn't a thaw in sight.

Cord's embittered accusations had wounded Stacy deeply. She wasn't able to discount them or shrug them aside.

It was impossible to ignore the things he had said by chalking them off to frustration; her feelings had been hurt too severely for that.

If he believed any portion of what he said, he couldn't possibly love her as she loved him. And that was the cruelest blow of all. Pride wouldn't let her go to him and try to undo the damage their heated argument had done.

Nor was she going to pretend that the traumatic scene had not taken place. If there was any tearing down of the barrier to be done, the first move would be made by Cord, not by her.

The music filtering through the closed door followed Stacy as she walked out the front door, stopping when she shut it securely behind her. It wasn't as easy to block out the haunting memory of Cord's unfounded accusations.

The pickup truck was parked in the driveway. Travis was kneeling beside the red tricycle on the sidewalk and Josh was beside him supervising the tightening of the handlebars.

Both had glanced up at the closing of the front door. Stacy forced the strained line of her mouth into a smile of greeting.

"If you start adjusting all of his toys to Josh's personal satisfaction, Travis, he'll never give you a minute's peace," she declared, teasing her son's near obsession for things to operate smoothly, a trait of his father's.

"I don't mind," Travis insisted with a slow smile, straightening to his full height. He ruffled the mop of shining black hair on Josh's head. "After all, a person can't steer a tricycle properly if there's too much play in the handlebars, right?"

"Right." Josh bobbed his head emphatically.

"It's no wonder he's becoming spoiled," Stacy sighed, but with loving indulgence. "Everyone on the ranch caters to him."

She glanced pointedly at her son. "Have you thanked Travis for fixing your tricycle? He wasn't obliged to do it."

White teeth bit into his lower lip as Josh cast a quick sideways look at the tall man. "Thank you, Travis," hurriedly expressing the gratitude prompted by her words.

"You're welcome," Travis rejoined.

Stacy breathed in deeply. "We'd better be going," she said to Travis. Then to Josh, "You behave yourself."

"Can't I come along?" he frowned.

"Not this time." She shook her dark head in a definite refusal. "And you stay right here in the house yard so Maria won't have to worry about where you are."

"Ah!" Josh grumbled, grimacing at the sidewalk. "Travis said there were two new colts in the barn. Can't I even go down and see them?"

"No, you can wait until after lunch and we'll go down to see them together. In the meantime you stay here where Maria can keep an eye on you. Do you understand?" Stacy repeated.

"Yeah," he mumbled.

"Yes what?" She prompted a more respectful reply.

"Yes, ma'am, I'll stay here" was his unenthusiastic response.

"I'll be back around lunchtime," she told him, and walked toward the pickup truck with Travis following her.

"He's quite a boy," Travis commented as he slid behind the wheel.

"Yes, he is," Stacy agreed quietly with a note of pride in her voice.

At the starting of the engine, she waved goodbye to Josh. The sight of the small figure watching her leave made her heart ache afresh. For Cord to think she wanted to leave him because of his confinement was one thing, but for him to accuse her of wanting to leave their son as well was unforgivable.

Hopelessness slumped her shoulders. Her elbow rested on the threshold of the truck window, the knuckles of her hand pressed fiercely on her trembling lips. She stared out of the window, her mind registering nothing that her eyes saw.

"I wish you hadn't let Cord talk you out of getting away for a few days," said Travis after several minutes of silence.

"What?" Her head jerked toward him in surprise and confusion.

Briefly his dark gaze left the rutted track to meet her stunned look of question. "Josh told me about it while I was fixing his tricycle," he explained. "I filled the odd parts in myself."

"How . . . how much did he tell you?" Stacy faltered.

"That he overheard the two of you arguing the other day about your leaving." They were approaching a fence gate and Travis geared the truck down. "Josh said that Cord refused to let you go."

When his gaze again swung toward her, Stacy averted her head, unwilling to meet his discerning look. He was much too perceptive.

"I see," she murmured the noncommittal remark.

"This is one time you should have stood your ground, Stacy," he observed grimly. "You need a break from the pressure of the ranch and Cord. Everything in general."

Stacy had two options. One was to deny that she had been the one to suggest to Cord that she wanted to get away for a few days. But that would mean explaining how Josh had misunderstood the argument. The second choice was to let Travis believe that she had asked Cord and he had refused to agree to a short vacation. She chose the second, not wanting to discuss the real argument that was still so very painful.

"I suppose I should have." The deliberately indifferent agreement was offered as Travis braked the truck to a stop at the fence gate. Immediately she lifted the door handle. "I'll open it."

Hopping quickly from the cab of the truck, she walked to the gate, unlatched it and swung it open for Travis to drive through. When the rear of the truck had cleared the gate, she closed it securely and walked back to the passenger side. With her fingers crossed that the subject was ended, she climbed back into the truck. For nearly a mile, there was silence.

"You didn't ask Cord if you could go away for a few days, did you?"

Travis stared at the ranch road, a grimness about his mouth.

Out of the corner of her eye, Stacy studied him, the strongly etched profile and the silvery streak of hair visible beneath the band of his Stetson hat. His perception was too acute. When his keen gaze swung to her, she looked away.

"What makes you say that?" She tried to sound casual.

"You've been too adamant about leaving Cord," he replied. "And if you had changed your mind, you can be as stubborn as he is. You wouldn't have let him dissuade you. That means Josh didn't understand the argument, did he?"

"Does anyone really understand arguments or how they get started?" Stacy responded ambiguously.

"Very seldom," Travis admitted. "Do you want to talk about it?"

Her shoulders lifted in a shrugging sigh. "Cord was just a little more unreasonable than usual, that's all."

"Was it his suggestion that you should leave?" he asked quietly.

"Something like that," she answered, again noncommittally.

There was a frowning arch of a thick brow in her direction. "Don't tell me he gave in to a quixotic impulse that you should leave him permanently rather than be tied to a supposed invalid the rest of your life?"

"Actually—" her mouth twisted wryly "—he believed that that was what I felt and what I wanted. He was reminding me of our marriage vows—in sickness and in health,'' her own paraphrase slipped out, "for bitter or worse.''

"I don't believe it!'' The words came out in an explosion of disgust.

"Unfortunately, it's true,'' she murmured.

"How—'' Travis began in controlled anger.

"Please,'' Stacy interrupted in a strained voice. "I really don't want to talk about it. It won't change anything.''

"I could certainly go talk to Cord and straighten him out on a few facts,'' he declared through clenched teeth.

"No,'' she refused his suggestion immediately. "I shouldn't have told you about the argument.''

"You didn't—Josh did.''

"That's a fine point since I explained what it was really about,'' Stacy smiled ruefully. "I shouldn't have. Our personal problems are something that Cord and I will have to work out alone.''

At the conclusion of her statement, they both lapsed into silence. It wasn't broken until they reached the noon holding ground for the cattle drive. Then their conversation was centered around the spring calf crop, the drive, the condition of the pastures and the water levels of the various wells.

When the main herd topped a distant crest, Stacy's mind wandered from the conversation between Travis and Ike, the trail boss. The dusty haze that obscured the cattle and their faint lowing held Stacy in the trip of nostalgic memories of other drives. She remembered the first drive when she and Cord had been virtually at war with each other.

After they were married, they had sentimentally spent at least one night on the trail during the drive. Sharing a bedroll, they had lain beside their camp fire isolated from the main campground. They had laughed and teased each other about that first drive when she had accused him of being an arrogant tyrant and he had declared her to be a pampered, spoiled city girl.

Closing her eyes, Stacy could remember the way their laughter and soft voices had inevitably faded into silence. For a few minutes they would simply gaze into each other's eyes. In the few seconds before Cord would draw her into his arms, the stars had always seemed to grow brighter, just as if they knew what was on the minds of the two lovers below.

They had been so close, spiritually and physically. An invisible knife twisted inside Stacy at the knowledge that they were further apart now than they had ever been.

Suddenly she wished she hadn't felt the necessity to personally check on the cattle drive. The bittersweet memories from previous ones were just too overwhelming.

Moving away from the windmill and its watering tank, Stacy joined the conversation between Travis and the trail boss, needing to lose herself in the present in order to forget the past. It was not an altogether successful attempt, she realized when Travis suggested some time later that they should be getting back to the ranch house. Her relief was too great.

Travis reversed the pickup onto the ranch road as the remuda vans arrived with fresh horses for the riders. During the drive back to the ranch house, Stacy felt his gaze dwelling on her several times. Yet, invariably when he spoke, the subject was only ranch business.

A small economy car was parked in the house driveway when they arrived. Stacy gazed at it curiously, not remembering for a brief instant that Paula Hanson, the physiotherapist, was expected today. There was an odd mixture of anxiety and hope that the woman was here.

"Do you suppose that's the therapist's car?" Travis stopped the pickup behind it.

"I imagine so," Stacy nodded. "I don't know of anyone else who was expected today."

Her hand gripped the door handle and hesitated before opening it. "Why don't you join us for dinner tonight, Travis?"

Brown eyes studied her thoughtfully. It wasn't uncommon for Travis to have dinner with them. Stacy had invited him often.

"What is Cord's attitude toward her?" He ignored her invitation for the moment.

She glanced at the door handle. There was no sense hiding the truth. Cord would be quick enough to tell it if the occasion arose.

"He's nearly convinced himself that it will be a waste of time." She was afraid Cord's opinion was more definite than that.

"So you want me to act as a buffer tonight?" There was an understanding quirk of his mouth.

"Something like that," Stacy smiled faintly. "I would like to make Miss Hanson's first night here as cordial as possible."

"She isn't married?" Travis questioned.

"No." Stacy shook her head negatively.

"Then I'll be there," he said, winking.

Despite his teasing inflection, there was a lack of any real interest in the woman's apparent eligibility. Stacy was reminded again of the heartbreak Travis concealed.

"Thanks." She opened the cab door and stepped out. "Is seven too early for you?"

"I can make it," he assured her as he shifted the truck into gear.

With a saluting wave of one finger, he pulled around the car and started toward the ranch buildings beyond the house. Stacy glanced at the lime-green economy car again and walked toward the house. Unconsciously she squared her shoulders as she walked through the front door.

In the living-room arch, she paused, staring at the woman seated on the sofa. Her hair was ash blond and long, swept away from her forehead and secured at the nape of her neck with a knotted scarf in a blue silk print.

Slacks of azure blue covered her long legs. Cajun's graying muzzle was resting near the toe of her white sandals. A sleeveless knit top in the same shade of blue as her slacks revealed a set of wide shoulders. The woman's stature was definitely one that could be described as Junoesque.

"Well, Mrs. Harris?" Paula Hanson spoke clearly when Stacy's slow study was completed. "Do you think I can handle him?"

She smiled slowly, and the action suddenly made Stacy forget that the woman's features were too forceful. The line of her brow was too straight. There was a slight crook in her nose and her chin jutted out from a strong jaw.

But the smile brought an animation to the face, a smile that was without guile. Even the woman's blue eyes seemed to sparkle a bit.

"What?" Stacy asked, forgetting the question that had just been put to her.

Paula Hanson's expression immediately became serious again as she rose to her feet, confirming Stacy's estimation that she was tall.

"You are Mrs. Harris, aren't you?" She tipped her head to one side, an end of her silk print scarf trailing over one shoulder.

"Yes, I'm Stacy Harris," she asserted with a quick smile. She walked into the living room, extending a hand toward the woman. "You obviously are Paula Hanson. I'm sorry I wasn't able to be here when you arrived."

"It's all right, I understand." Long fingers firmly clasped Stacy's hand in greeting. "Ma-

ria—that is your housekeeper's name, isn't it—
showed me my room and helped me settle in.
She indicated that you would be back for
lunch.''

"I hope everything is all right." But Stacy
had noticed the omission of any reference to
Cord. Hadn't they met yet?

"It's fine," Paula insisted.

She sat back on the sofa and reached for a
glass filled with red liquid and ice cubes that
was sitting on an end table. "Tomato juice
with a dash of Tabasco," she identified the
contents with dry amusement in her voice.
"Maria wanted to fix me something stronger,
but I didn't want you to think you suddenly
had a lush living in your home."

Stacy's smile became genuine and relaxed,
her faint wariness toward the stranger leaving.
"You're welcome to something stronger if you
like," she assured her.

"Do you think I'll need it?" she asked
Stacy.

A straight brow arched slightly as Paula's
gaze swung pointedly in the general direction
of the master bedroom.

"You haven't met—" Stacy breathed in
deeply "—my husband yet, have you?"

"No." Her gaze ricocheted from Stacy to study the clear cubes in her glass. "I have the feeling that he would like to ignore me as if I were a bad dream, in the hopes that I'll go away."

Stacy didn't attempt to deny the comment. "He is aware that you have arrived, isn't he?"

"Oh, yes," the physiotherapist confirmed. "Maria knocked on his door and told him, but he was somewhat unexcited about the news."

"I'm sorry—"

"There's no need to apologize," Paula Hanson hastened to interrupt. "Bill—Dr. Buchanan—explained the situation. Believe me, it's nothing I haven't encountered before."

Stacy turned. "I'll see if he'll join us for lunch."

"Don't bother on my account," the woman shrugged indifferently and sipped at the tomato juice. "He has to come out of the room sooner or later."

Looking over her shoulder at the blond-haired woman, Stacy felt confused by her attitude of unconcern and disinterest toward her patient.

"I thought you would want to meet Cord as soon as possible," she explained.

"There's time enough to beard the lion without doing it on an empty stomach," Paula Hanson declared dryly. "I tend to speak very bluntly, Mrs. Harris. So I don't intend to offend you when I say that all I've learned so far about your husband makes me believe that he'll be an abominable patient. I don't mind putting off meeting him for a few hours."

"I think you might be right." Stacy's lips twitched with amusement as she pivoted back toward the woman.

How long had it been since she had found humor in the situation? A very long time, if ever, she was sure. She had the feeling that she needed Paula Hanson's caustic wit as much as Cord needed her professional help.

"And please, call me Stacy," she added.

"Thank you, I will." The blonde leaned over and scratched behind the ears of the German shepherd lying near her feet. "And what would be this fellow's name?"

"Cajun." At the sound of his name coming from his mistress's lips, the dog thumped his tail against the floor and gazed adoringly at Stacy. "He seems to like you," she observed.

Again there was the dry curve of Paula Hanson's mouth. "All manner of beasts end up liking me."

The innuendo to Cord was not missed by Stacy. It was also a prophetic-sounding statement that she hoped would come true. Now that she had met Paula Hanson, Stacy didn't feel any of the jealousy that had been her initial reaction. Already the physiotherapist was like a breath of fresh air in a house that had become stagnant with bitterness.

Maria's plump figure rolled into the living room. "Lunch will be ready in a few minutes," she announced.

"Thank you," Stacy smiled, then glanced toward the dining room. "Where's Josh? Have you called him to wash yet?"

"He is outside. I fixed him a picnic lunch," the housekeeper explained. "What about Mister Cord? Is he coming to the table or should I fix him a tray?"

"You'll have to ask him. I haven't spoken to him since I came back," Stacy answered.

As the housekeeper's rolling walk carried her toward the master bedroom, Stacy turned to the blonde sitting on the sofa. "It might be a good thing that I made it back for lunch or you could have been eating your first meal here alone. Have you met our son, Josh, yet?"

Paula Hanson nodded that she had. "He was playing outside when I drove in. That boy is going to be breaking women's hearts when he grows up. I like almost all children, but he's a real charmer."

"Like his father was." The smile suddenly faded from Stacy's lips as she realized she had used the past tense. But it had been a very long time since Cord had been charming about or toward anything.

"My specialty is ill-tempered brutes. I'm accustomed to them snarling instead of charming, so don't feel self-conscious about the fact, Mrs. H—Stacy," Paula Hanson corrected. "It's my job, I hope, to change them back to what they were."

Stacy couldn't respond to that. Too many of her prayers were riding on those same thoughts. Instead she smiled weakly in acknowledgement of the comment.

"Would you excuse me, Miss Hanson?" she apologized, expressively rubbing her hands together. "I'm dusty from the drive. I'll have a wash and join you at the table in a few minutes."

"Fine," the blonde agreed.

Stacy was climbing the stairs to her room when Maria stepped out of the master bedroom, closing the door behind her. Stacy didn't pause to ask if Cord was joining them for lunch.

As Paula had said, he was trying to ignore the physiotherapist's presence in the house, and the best way to do that was to remain in his room. Stacy sighed at his stubbornness.

CHAPTER SIX

As SHE started down the steps to rejoin Paula Hanson, Stacy saw the back of Cord's wheelchair as it disappeared into the dining room, and she paused in surprise. She had been certain he would insist on having a lunch tray in his room. Her heart quickened at the thought that he might have changed his mind about the new therapy.

Hurrying down the stairs, she entered the living room as Cord wheeled his chair into the dining room. He stopped just inside the archway, obviously gazing at the blonde. For some reason Stacy hesitated for a moment, wanting to witness the meeting unseen. Unconsciously she held her breath, able to see his carved profile.

"So you're the miracle worker," he commented in a low, cynically mocking tone. His skepticism hadn't relented an inch and Stacy's bubble of hope was pricked.

"So you're the cripple," Paula Hanson returned the dry challenge.

Cord's nostrils flared whitely. "That's right," he agreed sharply. "And I'm likely to remain one, so you might as well plan on leaving."

"One of the advantages of my position," Paula replied smoothly, "is that once I'm assigned to a case, only the doctor in charge tells me when to leave. I don't take orders from you, Mr. Harris. In fact, the opposite is true. You take orders from me."

"Like hell I will!" A muscle was jumping along his jaw.

"Oh, you will," the blonde assured him in a silky voice. "You see, your muscles are weak from sitting all day in a wheelchair, whereas I'm as strong as a horse. Plus I'm mobile and you're crippled. So if you don't obey orders, I'll make you."

"I doubt that," he jeered.

"I've tossed around bigger men than you," she said with a shrugging inflection.

Cord tipped his head to one side, raven black hair gleaming in the light. "I wouldn't think that would be something a woman would brag about." There was sarcastic emphasis on her gender. "Is it a defense mechanism because you haven't got what it takes to attract a man?''

"Cord!" Stacy was aghast that he could be so cruelly insulting. Paula Hanson was an attractive woman. She rushed into the dining room, stunned also that he was so lacking in manners as to be rude to a guest in their home. Her gaze swerved apologetically to Paula Hanson. "I'm sorry, Miss Hanson."

"Don't be." The blonde showed no sign that the barbed comment had stung. "I've received more cutting insults than his made by children. His words only reveal his own fear of being unable to attract the opposite sex when he's confined to a wheelchair."

"You're insolent!" Cord snapped savagely.

"I'm impertinent and sassy, too!" Paula returned quickly, yet showing no sign of anger. "So it won't do you any good to try to browbeat me because I'll give it back just as fast I get it."

The line of his mouth thinned forbiddingly. "You're fired!"

"You've forgotten something—you can't fire me. I don't work for you, I work for Dr. Buchanan," she reminded him.

"You've overlooked one fact," Cord responded with grim complacency. "All I have to do is discharge Bill from the case to get rid of you."

"Stop it!" Stacy protested angrily. "How can you throw away this chance simply because your stupid pride has got in the way, Cord?"

With a violent push, he propelled the chair away from Stacy toward the table.

"When are you going to admit that this whole therapy thing is a waste of time?" he demanded beneath his breath.

"When did time become such a valuable commodity?" Fire flashed in her brown eyes. "All you do all day is sit in your chair and watch the second hand move on your wristwatch. Since you haven't anything better to do, you might as well try the therapy. You certainly don't have anything to lose."

"That's a valid point, Mr. Harris," Paula inserted as Cord glared at Stacy. "Although I doubt that you have the guts to admit it. But take your time about thinking it over. I don't object to spending a few days' paid vacation in your home while you do. Eventually I get bored doing nothing, though, don't you?" she challenged with arching sweetness.

"Don't try to put words in my mouth," warned Cord.

"If I did, I'd make you eat them," the blonde shrugged.

He pivoted the wheelchair toward Stacy.

"Get her out of here," he growled. "I've gone through enough hell without enduring a pain in the neck like her."

Outraged by his statement, Stacy stared at him in disbelief. But Paula only laughed at his derogatory comment.

"Haven't you learned that it doesn't do any good to lose your temper? Your wife or I might find it and give it back to you tenfold."

"One more remark out of you and I'll throw you out of this house myself!" Cord muttered.

Paula was standing several feet to the side. She walked to a point two feet in front of his wheelchair and placed her hands on her hips. Five foot eight in her stockinged feet, she towered above him.

"Why don't you do that, Mr. Harris?" she said in an agreeing voice. "Why don't you get out of that wheelchair and do it? *If* you think you're man enough?" His hands gripped the arms of the metal chair in impotent rage. "But you can't, can you?" she smiled slowly.

The harsh line of his mouth was compressed tightly, a black rage spreading over his dark features. He wheeled the chair around and rolled it toward the green telephone on the bureau.

"Don't bother to telephone Dr. Buchanan," Paula said quietly as he picked up the receiver. "If you take him off the case now, your wife can simply hire him back with the claim that you aren't capable of making the decision yourself. You're stuck with me, Mr. Harris."

Cord glared at Stacy, daring her to take sides against him. "I would do it, Cord," she stated emphatically.

He slammed the receiver back in its cradle. "I should have known I could not trust you," he snapped at Stacy.

"Look at it this way, Mr. Harris," Paula reasoned. "If after a few weeks of therapy, you're able to get out of that wheelchair, think of the satisfaction you'll have in throwing me out. Surely that's something you can look forward to?"

"It would be a joy," Cord declared through clenched teeth.

"Good. That's settled," the blonde nodded, and walked toward the table. "Now why don't you run along to your room like a good little boy? A meal always tastes better when there isn't a pouty child at the table."

"I'll be damned if I will," he breathed harshly.

"You'll have to behave yourself if you stay here." Her mouth quirked in a mocking smile. "Remember, I'm the one who's boss and you're the one who takes orders."

Stacy watched Cord's blazing dark eyes bore into the tall blonde, but Paula's serenely challenging composure didn't falter one whit. After crackling seconds, he propelled the chair angrily from the room. Stacy wasn't deceived that he was obeying the order. He was simply leaving before he gave in to the urge to kill.

"Whew!" Paula breathed with a silent laugh when he was out of hearing. "I thought I was going to need a whip and a chair there at the last to keep him at bay. He's a hell of a man."

The long clump of ash-blond hair brushed back and forth between her shoulder blades as she shook her head in respectful admiration.

A lump entered Stacy's throat as she gazed at the point where Cord had disappeared. "He was," she murmured in quiet agreement.

The rude, embittered man was not the same one she had married, nor even the arrogant, mocking tyrant that she had first met.

"Not was," Paula corrected. "He is a hell of a man. My problem is to channel all that ferocity and spirit into the exercises."

Sighing, she pulled out a chair and sat down at the table. "There went my resolve to stop falling in love with my patients."

Stacy stared at her incredulously. "I beg your pardon?" She couldn't have heard correctly.

Round blue eyes returned her look. "You might as well know it up front that I end up falling in love with my patients. I just can't keep from getting involved with them. Admittedly—" an impish light entered her eyes "—most of them haven't entered their teens yet. So my feelings have seldom been reciprocated except on the most platonic level. Considering everything your husband has to offer, I know I won't be immune to him." Paula paused, tipping her head to one side. "Do you want to reconsider taking me off the case, Stacy? I'll understand if you do. I would certainly be jealous of any woman who came near him if he was my husband. Not that I'll ever make a fool of myself and let him see the way I feel."

Stacy's mind ran through a whole gamut of thoughts as she hesitated before answering. There was admiration for the blonde's honesty, the knowledge that she instinctively liked Paula, and confidence that she had the ability to help Cord.

Also, there was the fear that Cord might fall in love with her. Patients had fallen in love with their nurses before and Stacy was not secure anymore, not after the last few weeks.

"No, I won't reconsider," she said finally, refusing to give into the selfish fear. "I want you to stay."

"I'm glad you thought about that before answering," Paula stated decisively. "Because I'm going to need your trust as much as I need his. I don't want to divide my energies by fighting for it from the two of you."

"Don't worry," Stacy smiled faintly. "Besides, I've invited our foreman to dinner tonight. He happens to be a tall, dark and handsome bachelor. Maybe we can channel your emotions to him instead of Cord."

"That's an idea," Paula laughed good-naturedly. "Ah, here comes Maria with lunch," she said, glancing up as the house-

keeper came from the kitchen. "I'm afraid
that as well as being as strong as a horse, I also
have the appetite of one."

True to her word, Paula cleaned her plate
with the gusto of one who enjoys good food.
Josh wandered into the dining room a few
minutes before Maria served a fresh fruit with
cheese dessert and succeeded in wheedling a
second helping from the housekeeper.

"You promised to take me to see the baby
colts, mom," he reminded Stacy between
spoonfuls.

"As soon as we have all finished with
lunch," she agreed.

"Would you like to come too, Paula?" he
asked brightly. "They've just been borned."

"The colts were just born," Stacy corrected
his grammar.

"That's what I said." He looked at her
blankly.

"And did you ask Miss Hanson's permission to call her by her first name?" Stacy inserted.

"She said I could," he nodded, and glanced
at the blonde for confirmation.

"I did tell him he could."

The slow smile spread across Paula's strong
features again.

"I'm accused often enough about being an old maid without a little boy calling me Miss Hanson. Please, you call me Paula, too, Stacy."

"You're welcome to come to the stables with us if you would like to," Stacy repeated Josh's offer.

"I would like to," she agreed. "I'm a native-born Texan, but the truth is I've never been on an honest-to-goodness ranch before. A few ranch-type farms, but nothing ever of this size."

"Josh and I will give you a grand tour, won't we, Josh?"

"You bet!" His bowl was scraped clean. He let the spoon clatter on the bottom as he hopped from the chair. "We can show you everything. We've got sheep and goats and horses and cattle and— Can you ride?" He interrupted his list with a quick question.

"Sorry, I don't know the front end of a horse from the back." The blonde lifted her hands palm upward, hiding her smile at his excitement.

"The back is where the tail is," he frowned at her ignorance.

"You'll have to show me." Paula offered him her hand and he grasped it immediately, eager to be off on the tour of the ranch.

"At a walk, though, Josh. I'm not as young as you are."

"You two go ahead." Stacy waved them on. "I want to have a word with Maria. I'll meet you outside in a few minutes."

During the tour of the ranch, Paula continually expressed her amazement at the size of the operation. Seeing it through a stranger's eyes, Stacy was actually a little stunned by it herself. She had become so familiar with it over the years that she had taken it for granted.

"You're really in charge of all this?" Paula queried again as she paused on the rise leading to the house. She looked back at the ranch property sweeping endlessly to the horizon.

"Yes." Stacy smiled, bemused by the fact, as well. "With Travis McCrea, our foreman. I'm not so foolish that I think I could run it without his help."

"I didn't mean anything chauvinistic by that remark," the blonde hastened. "There isn't any reason why a woman isn't just as capable as a man of operating a ranch. I was just wondering what your husband's reaction is to it."

"Cord's?" Stacy frowned in faint bewilderment. "I'm not sure I know what you mean."

"I was thinking it must have deflated his ego a bit to have everything running so smoothly without him. As proud and independent as he is, I bet he wished it had fallen apart—secretly at least."

Her thoughtful gaze swung to Stacy, a questioning light blue. "Or has he taken part in some of the decisions?"

Remembering how Cord had accused her of patronizing him, Stacy shook her head and looked away. "Travis and I have tried to involve him in the running of the ranch, but he refused to take any interest."

"I see," Paula mused absently.

"Aren't you coming?"

Josh was waiting impatiently at the sidewalk, anxious to enter the house and have the afternoon snack of milk and cookies he knew Maria would have ready for him.

"I appreciate your taking the time to show me around," said Paula as they jointly turned to accompany Josh into the house. "It was a revelation for me. I hope it didn't interfere too much with your schedule?"

"It didn't," Stacy assured her. "The heat of the afternoon I generally spend in the office doing the book work after devoting a couple of hours to Josh.'' She glanced at her watch as Paula opened the front door. ''I still have time to do the biggest share of the book work before dinner. Incidentally, I've asked Travis to come at seven and Maria is planning dinner for seven-thirty.''

''While you're working, I can take all the time I need to get ready for dinner and—'' the blonde laughed with self-mockery ''—I hope, impress your bachelor foreman tonight!''

The door to the master bedroom was ajar. As Stacy was about to respond to Paula's comment, Cord's voice barked her name.

''Stacy!''

In the rolling arc of her gaze to Stacy, Paula's blue eyes seemed to say that the beast had roared a summons for her presence at his throne. It was an expressively mocking look that made Stacy smile.

''Excuse me. I'll see you later, Paula,'' she murmured, and moved toward the partially opened door.

''Where have you been?'' Cord demanded when she entered the room.

''Josh wanted to see the new colts after lunch. And since Miss Hanson had never been on a working ranch before, I took her on a tour." It was difficult to reply calmly and keep the edge of temper from showing at his peremptory tone.

"That viper-tongued witch!" he jeered.

"She was no more rude and insulting than you were," Stacy reminded him sharply. "If you'd seen her this afternoon with Josh, you would know how terribly you misjudged her. She was completely at ease with him, more natural than a lot of parents are with their own children. Miss Hanson knows exactly how to handle children."

"Is that some snide endorsement of her ability to handle me?" he asked. His mouth thinned sardonically.

"It wasn't," Stacy flashed. "But I won't deny that you behaved like a boorish brat this noon. You deserved to be put down."

"You made it very clear earlier that you'd sided against me." His gaze narrowed with piercing censure. "Is this your way of taking revenge because I won't allow you to go away?"

"Why do you have to be so unreasonable?" she protested bitterly. "It wasn't a question of taking sides—I was doing what I believed was right for you. That was my only motive." She avoided the battleground of disclaiming she had ever suggested she wanted to go away.

"Since it's my life and my body, I should have some decision in what's done with it," declared Cord. "Not you."

"As long as your life affects mine and Josh's, I do have a right," Stacy asserted.

"I didn't realize you were so bored with your life here that you would welcome the company of that blond viper."

He wheeled his chair to the window and apparently unable to find a valid argument to her comment, he had altered the subject instead.

"I'm too busy to be bored. Tired, yes, but not bored," she sighed. "Miss Hanson is a working guest, but she still is a guest in our home. I'd like you to remember that tonight at dinner and treat her accordingly."

"Do you mean she gave me permission to come to the table?"

Cord glanced over his right shoulder, a contemptuous lift to a black brow. "Am *I* supposed to feel honored that she's willing to endure my presence at the table? Or grateful that she didn't order me to stay in my room without supper?"

His fingers ground into the arm of the chair. "That woman really has gall, ordering me around in my own home!"

"She would have to have gall to stand up to you," Stacy returned. "I don't want to quarrel about this with you anymore—I have more constructive things to do with my time. I've invited Travis to dinner tonight. He'll be here around seven."

"What did you do?" Cord breathed contemptuously. "Turn tonight's meal into a dinner party for that witch? Why didn't you roll out the red carpet and hire a brass band?"

"Her name is Paula Hanson," she corrected tightly. "Would you please remember that? And it isn't exactly a dinner party. I hope it will be just a cordial evening without any embarrassing scenes."

"Now I embarrass you." There was scorning amusement in his voice. "What comes next, Stacy? Will you become sick of the sight of me?"

"For heaven's sake, Cord!" she exclaimed in disgust. "Don't twist everything I say. I only mean that I didn't want you hurling any more insults at Miss Hanson during dinner this evening."

"Is that why you invited Travis?" he mocked. "Is he to provide Miss Hanson—" stressing the proper name sarcastically "—with some male companionship or to keep the conversation on safe topics."

"Both, I hope," Stacy agreed.

"For an instant, there was silence.

Then Cord sighed wearily, all of the sarcasm and bitterness seeming to flow out of him. He rubbed the back of his neck for several seconds.

"I didn't call you in her to taunt you, Stacy," he muttered thickly. "I don't even know how it got started. I lash out at everyone these days."

"Why did you call me?" she asked, trying to adjust to the change in the atmosphere.

"I was worried about you. You were gone longer than I thought you would be and Maria said Josh was with you. I—"

Cord hesitated, still staring out the window. "Don't worry about tonight. I'll be pleasant to your miracle worker."

"Thank you, Cord," Stacy murmured, biting her lip at the cynical tone of his voice. "If you need me, I'll be in the study. I have some book work to do before dinner."

The congenial atmosphere that dominated the evening meal was a welcome change from the taut, uneasy silences of previous ones.

It was due in part to the immediate rapport between Travis and Paula, an instant and mutual liking and respect for each other.

The polite phrases of two strangers meeting were bypassed, eliminating the tension of a getting-acquainted period.

Conversation at the dinner table was centered mainly between Travis and Paula, with Stacy joining in frequently. Paula's brief tour of the ranch that afternoon had whetted her curiosity to learn more about the workings of the ranch and especially the cattle drive being carried out. Travis obligingly explained it to her.

Cord, who had grown to detest any discussion of the ranch operation, exhibited commendable restraint and remained silent during much of the dinner. Covertly Stacy studied his expression, trying to discern some small crack in his mask of indifference. Nothing revealed that he listened as eagerly as Paula did to the activities going on now.

There didn't seem to be a glimmer of interest. Cord was keeping to his promise to be pleasant this evening. More than that Stacy couldn't read into his silence no matter how much she wanted to try.

She attempted to feel grateful that he wasn't sniping away at the blond physiotherapist, but there wasn't much comfort in that. Stacy was becoming as difficult to satisfy as Cord. She sighed inwardly as Maria cleared the dessert dishes and brought in the coffee.

A cup was set in front of Cord.

"No!" he sputtered. The word seemed to explode from him, almost involuntarily. With suppressed violence he pushed his chair away from the table. Controlling the faint snarl in his voice with an effort, he muttered, "I'll have my coffee on the veranda, Maria."

He did not invite anyone to join him as he wheeled his chair toward the sliding glass doors. The omission was too blatant for any of them to miss.

Paula made a slight face and murmured. "Why didn't he come right out and say he didn't want our company? I could have taken the hint."

Travis chuckled softly at her dry wit. Stacy smiled stiffly. There was no point in apologizing to them or making excuses for Cord's behavior. Yet something inside her wouldn't let him exile himself to the veranda alone.

Glancing at Maria, who was setting Cord's cup back on the tray, Stacy said, "I'll have my coffee on the veranda, too, Maria." Briefly she nodded to Travis and Paula. "Excuse me," she said, and rose from her chair.

CHAPTER SEVEN

THE NIGHT air was sultry from the afternoon's heat. The starfire shimmering from the sky cast soft shadows on the whitewashed arches of the veranda.

Cord murmured a terse "thank you" when Maria set the tray on a table near his wheelchair. His gaze riveted itself on the two cups sitting on the tray, recognizing the significance of them and knowing he wasn't alone.

Stacy paused behind him, feeling the invisible crackle of electricity in the still air. Her heels clicked loudly on the cobblestones as she ignored his silent demand to leave and walked to a chaise longue beside him.

"What are you doing out here?" he muttered impatiently, then continued without allowing her an opportunity to reply. "If you've come to tell me that I've rudely left our guests, you can save your breath." His voice curled sarcastically around the word "guests." "If I'd stayed inside, I doubt if I would have kept my promise. So be grateful for a small show of bad manners.''

"I am.'' Stacy leaned back in her chair and sipped at her coffee, refusing to respond to his baiting tone.

The starlight glittered over the tightly clenched line of his jaw. "Shouldn't you go back inside with our guests?'' There was a savage undercurrent in his biting mockery. "One of us should be in there to entertain them.''

"Travis isn't exactly a guest,'' she replied evenly. "He can keep Paula company for a while.''

"You make it sound as if he's practically a member of the family instead of the fore-man,'' Cord jeered with disdain.

"I guess I do think of him in that way,'' Stacy admitted. "I don't believe you realize how much help he's been to us through all this.''

"To you, you mean,'' he corrected. His mouth quirked bitterly. "Do you confide all your troubles to him and cry on his shoulder?''

"I don't cry on anyone's shoulder.''

She was too independent to do that and she knew it, even if at times she wanted to pour out her troubles to someone. "The help I referred to that Travis had given us was shouldering the bulk of the ranch operation. I didn't mean help that he had personally given me," she explained.

Travis's knowledge of her problems was gleaned from what he had witnessed or guessed and not from any confessions from Stacy, regardless of Cord's accusation to the contrary.

"And you're so grateful for his assistance that you've left him in the house alone with that barracuda," Cord jeered.

Stacy breathed in deeply, fighting to control the spark of temper before it burst into flame. He seemed determined to incite an argument and she was just as determined not to oblige.

"Cord, I came out here for some fresh air," she said slowly and distinctly, "certainly not to become embroiled in a bitter dispute with you. If you don't want to enjoy the peace and quiet, then I'll move to another part of the veranda where I can."

His cup clinked loudly in its saucer. Stacy's heart thudded rapidly in the heavy silence that followed. It was not a desire for fresh air that had brought her outdoors but the sensation that Cord had wanted her company. She wanted his, but not if it meant arguing. She had endured all the embittered and angry exchanges that she could stand for one day.

Gradually the prickles at the back of her neck eased and Stacy relaxed, resting her head against the back of the chair cushion. Miles away, a coyote yipped. The sound echoed clearly to her ears.

Her thoughts drifted to the cattle drives as she gazed at the stardust sky. Somewhere out there a night rider was watching over the herd, taking his turn while others slept in bedrolls around the camp fire. A lump entered her throat as Stacy remembered again the nights she and Cord had camped out.

Eager to rid her mind of the haunting image, she focused her attention on the mechanics of the drive and Travis's recounting of the drive's success so far this year. It had been almost unbelievably smooth and without incident.

"It's a relief that the cattle drive is going so well." The absent comment was out before Stacy realized that it was her voice that had broken the silence.

Darting a quick, sideways glance at Cord, she held her breath. There wasn't any tightness to his smooth jawline that was usually present whenever any mention of the ranch's operation was made in his hearing.

He appeared relaxed and calm as he gazed heavenward at the stars.

The tensing of her nerves eased. Stacy decided he hadn't heard her inadvertent remark and breathed a silent sigh of relief. She let her gaze swing back to the stars.

"I can almost smell the smoke from the camp fire," Cord murmured softly.

The starlight seemed to glow more brilliantly, filling her brown eyes with hopeful light as his warm voice rolled caressingly over her. Hesitantly she glanced at him, wondered if he, too, was remembering the nights they had spent alone on the trail. The affirmative answer was in the glittering darkness of his gaze on her face.

No words were spoken as they gazed at each other. Sometime during the eternity of seconds, his wheelchair glided silently to the side of her chair. Stacy wasn't aware of its actual movement. She wasn't certain that Cord knew he had done it.

He was simply there, near enough that she could have touched him with only the slightest movement of her hand. But she didn't. His previous rejections of any physical contact with her were too painfully branded in her heart. Any touch or caress would come first from Cord or not at all.

As he remained motionless for several more seconds, Stacy quivered with the aching longing to be in his arms. He leaned forward, his hands clasping her rib cage to draw her toward him. She didn't need the assistance to move to the hard male line of his descending mouth.

The searing possession of his kiss burned the softness of her lips. Fire rocketed through her veins as she responded to his hungry demand. Her hands cupped the powerful line of his jaw, hard and firm beneath her fingers.

Too soon, his hands were decisively but slowly pushing her away from him. Her own hands retained the shape of his face, suspended in air, as Cord set her back in her chair. Unwillingly her lashes fluttered open. His eyes were black, fathomless pools of torture.

"Stacy, my life," Cord whispered with agony. "What am I doing? I'm destroying both of us. For bitter or worse, you said. But how much more bitter can either of us take?"

He turned away, his profile hardening into an unrelenting silhouette in the starlight. "God help me, I can't let you go. I'll never let you go!''

"Cord, I don't want to go," she murmured huskily. "I only want you to stop shutting me out. I want to share in your life."

A dark eyebrow arched with bitter cynicism. "I can't share. What is there for me to share? My wheelchair? It's my prison." His mouth twisted in sardonic amusement. "The wheelchair is my prison, yet I'm your jailer. I'll never let you go free."

"I don't want to be free," Stacy protested with a faint catch of pain in her voice.

"Do you know what I'm afraid of?" There was no humor in his chilling smile. "That some day you'll say that so often I'll finally believe you—even though I know it's not the truth."

"No." It was an inaudible denial, lost in a choked sob that Cord didn't hear.

There was a quiet swish of his wheels turning. Stacy's head was bowed so she didn't see him reenter the house. Her hands were clasped tightly in front of her in desperate prayer. Pain reverberated through her body, racking her muscles until she wanted to cry away the hurt, but she held the flood of tears in check.

It was several minutes before she was in sufficient control of herself to join Travis and Paula in the living room. A hand wearily pushed the hair away from her forehead as she walked into the house.

The sight of Cord in the living room brought her to an abrupt halt. She had been certain he would retreat to his bedroom.

The impregnable hardness of his gaze swept over her, noting the ravages of her storm within. A cigarette was in his hand, and the gray smoke outlined the ebony blackness of his hair.

Not a sound had betrayed Stacy's entrance into the living room, yet Paula glanced up, as if sensing a change in the atmosphere. Her azure eyes narrowed briefly on Stacy's wan cheeks, and a split second later a smile of warm greeting was rimming the blond woman's face.

"You're just in time, Stacy," Paula declared, darting a fleeting sideways glance at Travis. "I was just trying to find out more about this annual horse sale you have from Travis. He said you were in charge of that, and that it had been your personal project for the last several years."

"That's true."

Stacy started forward, grateful for the safe topic of conversation and the lack of any comment about where she had been. "What did you want to know about it?"

"Well, I—" Paula began.

"Isn't there something else we can discuss?" Cord interrupted with a snap. He ground his cigarette out in an ashtray, suppressing anger in the action.

There was a challenging tilt of the physiotherapist's head in his direction. "I was only going to ask Stacy what she was doing now—in connection with the sale."

"What difference does it make to you?" Cord met her look and returned the challenge.

"It doesn't make any difference to me," Paula shrugged. "I was just interested."

"Well, I'm not!" he retorted.

"Do you mean you're not interested in what goes on here at the ranch?" she asked with a long considering look.

"That's precisely what I mean," Cord replied sharply.

"I understood it was your ranch." Paula tapped a cigarette from the pack sitting on the table in front of her.

As she placed the filtered tip between her lips, Cord's gold lighter was there to touch a flame to the tobaccoed end. Stacy saw their gazes lock above the yellow flame.

"It was," he agreed, stressing the past tense. "Since my accident, Stacy and Travis have taken over the operation of it. It's not my affair anymore."

"Why?" Paula blew a stream of smoke into the air.

"They make all the decisions," was his answer.

"Why don't you, if it's your ranch?" she challenged.

"In case it hasn't occurred to you, Miss Hanson—" there was a sarcastic inflection in his voice "—it's difficult to oversee an operation of this size from a wheelchair."

"Difficult but not impossible, Mr. Harris," returning his cutting formality in kind. "Other men confined to wheelchairs have controlled holdings larger and more complex than yours."

A muscle leaped in his jaw, the only indication of his severely checked anger. "Really?" he drawled with indifference.

"When I first met you, I thought you were that kind of man," Paula continued. "It never occurred to me that you would let a woman rule your life, even if she is your wife. Of course—'' she shrugged nonchalantly ''—initially I thought you were a man.''

''Meaning?'' he demanded coldly.

''Surely I don't have to explain.'' Paula blinked her widened eyes. ''You're the one who's hiding behind your wife's skirt and letting her make all the decisions. You could hardly be described as the master of your own destiny.''

Stacy had apprehensively sunk her teeth into her lower lip at the insult to Cord's masculinity in Paula's last remark. She took a step forward, but Travis caught her eye and shook his head.

Stacy breathed in sharply in surprise when she saw Cord lean back in his chair and laugh silently, admittedly without humor.

''You're not opposed to hitting below the belt, are you?''

The grooves around his mouth deepened with satirical amusement as his gaze narrowed on his blond adversary.

''Why should I be?'' Paula countered. ''You don't seem to be bothered when you hurt people who care about you.''

Just in case Cord didn't understand her vague reference to Stacy, Paula glanced pointedly at her, dwelling on the lines of strain around her mouth and eyes.

Cord followed her look. There wasn't even a glimmer of guilt or remorse in his impassive features. He turned back to Paula, a suggestion of arrogance in the tilt of his head.

"You can do all the hitting below the belt that you want, Miss Hanson," he said calmly. "It doesn't bother me in the least. As for my wife—" his gaze slashed to Stacy; it's mockery chilled her "—Stacy and I understand each other. I'm perfectly aware of what she wants. I doubt very seriously, Miss Hanson, if you do. Now, I'll bid all of you good night and relieve you of my uncomfortable presence."

As he started to move his wheelchair forward, Paula suggested smoothly, "I think you're the one who is uncomfortable, Mr. Harris."

Cord paused, met her challenging glance, and smiled.

"I'm bored, but not uncomfortable." His smile deepened, carving grooves near his mouth. "As a matter of fact, Miss Hanson, I'm now beginning to realize that these little battles with you just might relieve my boredom.''

A silence followed his departure from the room, with all three pairs of eyes watching him leave. All of them were a bit stunned by his curious about-face and what it meant.

''Round two was a draw,'' Paula breathed finally. ''I think I'm going to have to be on my toes tomorrow morning if I expect to come out on top.''

''Cord isn't the type to let anyone else stay on top for long,'' Travis commented idly, unaware that he had spoken his thoughts aloud. ''He always lands on his feet, like a cat.''

''I hope I'm as agile,'' Paula tacked on thoughtfully.

An icy finger trailed down Stacy's spine and she shivered. Her world was being turned upside down and there seemed to be nothing she could do or say to put it right. Earlier Cord had called her his life. In the next breath, he had declared he didn't believe her when she said she never wanted to leave him.

Time was on her side and she could overcome that. But that wasn't what was making her blood run cold. It was his comment that Paula would provide a diversion to his boredom. Stacy was afraid of what that might mean. Cord was virtually a stranger to her. She didn't know him anymore.

A lump rose in her throat. Her stomach churned sickeningly, and rubbery legs threatened to give way beneath her. She swayed unsteadily, a hand pressing itself against the flat of her stomach to quell the convulsing muscles.

"I—I think I'll check on Josh."

She needed to escape, so she grabbed at the first logical excuse.

"Stacy."

Paula's voice checked her first awkward step from the room. "Before I forget, will you be here at the house tomorrow morning?"

"I—" She couldn't think. Tomorrow was an eternity away and her mind couldn't seem to focus on it.

"You mentioned something about going into town in the morning," Travis prompted gently.

"Oh, yes, of course," Stacy laughed brittlely, running a trembling hand along her temple. "I have to take the yearling list for the sales catalog to the printers in the morning." Her nerves were threadbare. "Was there something you wanted, Paula?"

"No." Paula inhaled briefly on her cigarette and snuffed it out in the ashtray. "I was going to start initiating your husband to his exercises and I just wondered where you would be."

"I can postpone going into town until the afternoon if you'd like me to help." The offer was made almost desperately as Stacy turned, her chestnut hair swinging silkily around her shoulders. She wanted to maintain any link with Cord regardless of how rusty the connection might be.

"Don't do that." The blonde shook her head.

"I don't mind. I—I want to help."

For the first time, Stacy noticed a flash of uncertainty in the woman's face. The blue eyes looked in her direction without looking directly at her.

"Actually, Stacy, it would be better if you weren't here—at least in the beginning," Paula hastily added. "I'm afraid you would be more of a distraction than a help, however good your intentions. The therapist-patient relationship is very important, especially in your husband's case. Besides, the first few days or more will probably be pretty rough on Cord. Caring about him the way you do, your instinct would be to try to make it easier for him. I'm sorry, but it's nothing personal.''

"I understand.''

Did she though? Stacy didn't know. There were so many things she didn't know or understand anymore. Not the least among them was Cord.

"Excuse me,'' she murmured, and this time made her exit from the room.

The next morning Stacy had genuinely intended to be gone from the house before Paula started her exercise and therapy program with Cord. But one minor interruption after another kept her in the study until half-past nine.

With the list in her hand of the yearling colts and fillies to be sold, Stacy walked out of the study. The door to the master bedroom was ajar. It drew her gaze like a magnet. A muffled exclamation of pain made her hesitate.

"Dammit, that hurts!'' she heard Cord mutter savagely.

"Well, dammit, it's supposed to,'' was the unruffled response from Paula. "It's going to hurt a lot more before we're through.''

"I don't like it when a woman swears,'' he retorted with a muffled undertone of discomfort.

"For once we share a similar viewpoint, Mr. Harris," Paula declared. "I find it offensive when a man swears."

Suddenly Stacy realized that she was eavesdropping. That realization was followed immediately by a niggling doubt that she had allowed herself to be detained at the house when she could have left earlier as planned.

With a guilty start, she hurried toward the front door before her presence was discovered.

The next day Stacy made certain that she succeeded in leaving the house early in the morning, not returning until lunchtime. Insecurity had allowed twinges of jealousy to enter her, and she overcompensated for them by staying away rather than turning into a suspicious, prying wife.

True to Paula's prediction, the first week was miserable. Stacy's self-imposed exile in the mornings had begun to make her feel like an intruder in her own home, as if she should ask permission whenever she wanted to spend any length of time there during the day.

The mental and physical exertion had made Cord ill-tempered. His moods varied from brooding silence to snarling sarcasm. It seemed to Stacy that she was his favorite target, although Paula received her fair share of his scathing remarks.

Maybe it only seemed that Cord singled Stacy out because her love gave him such an overwhelming power to hurt. Inwardly she cringed when his slashing tongue cut her heart to ribbons, but she didn't let her wounds show. She tried to mimic Paula by pretending his acid comments bounced off her as they appeared to bounce off Paula.

As her fork played with the tuna-salad stuffing of her tomato, Stacy searched for something to say. The heavy atmosphere at the lunch table was oppressive, induced by Cord's brooding silence. The prong of her fork made a scraping sound on the plate.

Jet dark eyes pierced her. "Are you going to eat that or just keep pushing it around on your plate?" Cord snapped.

His sudden attention disconcerted her. Awkwardly she laid the fork down and clasped her shaking fingers in her lap, out of sight of Cord's penetrating gaze.

"I'm not very hungry," she answered with forced calm.

"Then stop playing with your food," he growled.

Silence descended again. Stacy glanced at Paula, wondering how the blonde could be so indifferent to the brittle tension. Or was she simply a better actress than Stacy?

"How is the—the therapy coming along?" Stacy faltered over the question, again drawing Cord's gaze.

"Don't ask me, ask Paula." There was an arrogant flare of his nostrils in scorn. "She's supposed to be the expert."

The physiotherapist's knife sliced through the red tomato. "It's Miss Hanson to you, Mr. Harris," Paula corrected him smoothly. "When you become a person I can like and respect, then you have permission to call me Paula, but not before."

"Miss Hanson—" the strong line of his lip curled sarcastically over her name "—I don't particularly care whether you ever like me or not."

"And vice versa, Mr. Harris," Paula returned with a saccharine smile. When the blue eyes turned to Stacy, they held a twinkling light of mock despair. "To answer your question, Stacy, it's slow when you have to fight every inch of the way."

"Translated, that means a lot of pain and little progress," Cord inserted dryly.

"When did you become such an optimist, Cord?" Stacy's mouth curved into a humorless smile.

"What?" He looked at her blankly.

"You just admitted there was a little progress, which is better than none at all," she retorted.

He exhaled a short, angry breath. "Damned little," he muttered in a savage undertone. Almost instantly a black eyebrow arched in Paula's direction. "Pardon me, Miss Hanson."

"I'll be damned if I should, but I will, Mr. Harris." A smile twitched at the corners of her full mouth.

Jealousy flamed with emerald green fire inside Stacy at the exchange. Before it consumed her with its self-destructive force, she pushed her chair away from the table. The suppressed violence of her action nearly tipped over the glassware.

"Excuse me, I have work to do," she muttered as she started to flee from the surprised glances.

Inside the study, she shut the door and leaned against it. If she hadn't overheard their conversation the other day, she wouldn't have understood the teasing subtlety regarding swearing that had passed between Cord and Paula.

Now they were sharing secret jokes. In the green-eyed throes of her misery, she wondered what else they shared during all the mornings she left them alone.

She walked to the desk. At this time she knew she wouldn't be able to concentrate on paperwork. Her mind would be wondering what was going on in the rest of the house.

Her wide-brimmed Western hat was sitting on top of the letter basket where she had left it this morning. Picking it up, she hurried from the study and out of the house.

At the stable, Hank stared at her in astonishment. "Saddle the mare?" He repeated her request. "You want to go ridin' in the heat of the day?" He peered at her closely, his weathered face crinkled by the sun. "Are you all right, Miss Stacy?"

"Of course," she answered sharply. She sunk her teeth into her lip for an instant to check any further venting of frustration on Hank.

"If you're too busy, Hank, I'll saddle Candy Bar myself."

"I'll do it," he grumbled and shuffled toward the corral. But Stacy heard him mumble as he left, "Somebody around here is tetched in the head, and it ain't me!"

CHAPTER EIGHT

THE GREEN pickup truck rumbled down the lane toward the stables, slowing down as it approached Stacy walking toward the house. She waited until it stopped beside her, and smiled tiredly at the dark-haired man behind the wheel. His arm was crooked over the open window of the cab.

"Hello, Travis," she greeted him. "It seems like I haven't seen you for ages." He was the one person with whom she didn't feel she always had to be on her guard.

"We've both been pretty busy these last three days," he agreed. He kept the truck in gear, the engine idling eagerly.

"How are the preparations for the horse sale going?" he asked.

"Fine," Stacy nodded with a wry smile. "I think," she added the qualification.

"And Cord?" The brown eyes were thoughtful as they ran over her wholesomely attractive features, drawn and tired, the signs of weight loss visible in the accented hollows of her cheeks. "Paula has been here almost two weeks now. Has there been any improvement?"

"None that I know about," Stacy glanced self-consciously away.

The information hadn't been volunteered to her regarding Cord's progress, or lack of it. It had been on the tip of her tongue several times to put the question to Paula, but the very fact that Stacy hadn't been kept informed held her back.

"It takes time, I guess," Travis shrugged.

"Yes, of course," she agreed. "I was just going up to the house for lunch. Would you like to join me?"

He frowned curiously. "Won't Cord and Paula be there?"

"Sure," she smiled nervously.

It had been a slip of the tongue to say "me." The truth was that Stacy felt like the unwanted third at the table. The thought of Travis joining them for lunch had been a means of being included for once instead of feeling left out. She realized that it was all in her imagination, but she still felt uncomfortable.

"I'd like to," Travis hesitated, "but—"

"I understand," Stacy inserted, stretching her mouth into a smile. "Work," she offered him an excuse. "Another time."

"I'll hold you to it," he smiled, and the truck began rolling forward.

If only something had developed between Paula and Travis, Stacy sighed wistfully. But it hadn't. They were friendly toward each other but nothing more.

When her path was clear, she started toward the house again. The closer she got, the more taut her nerves became. Her throat and mouth were dry. The food would be tasteless again.

Lately she had had to force herself to eat, but the portions that she had succeeded in swallowing had been small.

"Hi, mom!"

Josh came racing down the sloping lawn toward her. Water glistened on his chest, browned by the sun. His red swimming trunks were plastered to his slender form. Shining wet hair gleamed as black as a raven's wing in the sunlight.

"You've been playing with the water hose again, I see," Stacy smiled indulgently.

"No, I've been swimming," he corrected her brightly.

The smile vanished completely.

"Joshua Stephen Harris!"

She grasped his shoulders and gave him a hard shake. "You've been told and told and told never to go swimming by yourself! You are not to be in that pool unless y—" Stacy had been about to say "your father or I," but she quickly changed it "—there's an adult in the pool with you. Now you can spend the afternoon in your room."

His dark eyes flashed resentfully at her.

"But daddy and Paula were in the pool with me!" he declared.

"I don't like it when you lie to me, Josh," scolded Stacy. Her frayed nerve ends had armed her temper with a short fuse.

"I am not lying. It's the truth!" Josh insisted. "We all went swimming together."

Her chestnut head tipped to one side in doubt. "Your father, too?" she questioned skeptically.

"Paula said it was 'therapy'—" he mispronounced the unfamiliar word "—to make daddy stronger. They've been swimming every day and today Paula said I could come in, too."

The brisk nod of his chin added a very definite "so there!" to the end of his explanation.

"I—" Stacy was flustered. She had heard of swimming used in therapy, but she hadn't realized Paula was employing it. "I didn't know. I'm sorry, Josh."

He accepted her apology somewhat sullenly, his lower lip jutting out in a pout.

She should have realized he wouldn't deliberately disobey her. Or if he did, he wouldn't brag about it. She was just too keyed up. She shouldn't have jumped on him without allowing him to make an explanation.

"I was wrong and I take back everything I said. Naturally you don't have to stay in your room this afternoon," she added.

Then trying to change the subject, she said, "Do you suppose Maria has lunch ready yet? Shall we go and see?"

A bare toe dug into a clump of grass. "I guess so," he agreed without enthusiasm.

But he didn't walk beside her. Instead he raced ahead, a faint droop to his shoulders. Her unwarranted anger had taken his enjoyment out of the morning swim and he wasn't going to let her forget it immediately. Knowing that she had been wrong only made Stacy feel worse.

If only Paula or Cord had mentioned the morning swims, Stacy defended her action silently, none of this would have happened. Resentment smoldered, as it had done in Josh.

Entering the house, Stacy walked directly toward the master bedroom. It was time she found out all that was going on in her house. She had a right to know what was being done, when, where, and why.

The door was opened. A half step through the frame, Stacy halted, stopped by the sight of Cord lying nearly half-naked on a sheet-draped table. A blue towel was wrapped around his waist. The narrow width of the towel revealed the rippling muscles of his shoulders and back, and the dark curling hair on his thighs and legs. Lying on his stomach, his head was resting on his hand, his face turned away from the door. Dampness changed his hair to midnight black, inclining it to wave.

Stacy's view was blocked by a tall, slender shape as a pair of strong hands began spreading a glistening oil all over Cord's naked back. Her gaze swept over the woman.

Ash-blond hair was swept on top of her head in a disheveled coil. Wet tendrils had escaped to curl attractively on the slender column of her neck. A white lace beach jacket veiled a two-piece swimming suit, revealing the stunning length of golden legs.

Long fingers supplely massaged Cord's back, polishing the bronzed tan of his skin with the oil. How unobservant she had been these past days, Stacy thought silently. Not once had she noticed the deepening shade of Cord's sunbrowned skin. Her pulse stirred at the virility stamped in the totally male figure. There was an ache in the pit of her stomach, a yearning emptiness that wanted to be filled.

Envy crushed her heart into a painful ball as Stacy watched Paula's hands moving with familiar intimacy over his naked back and shoulders. A cry of jealous anger rose in her throat that Paula, and not herself, was the one touching him, caressing him. Smothering the tortured sob with the back of her hand, Stacy retreated from the doorway on trembling legs.

It was either retreat or she would have raced into the room, screaming and clawing at Paula. The violence of her raging emotions dazed her. Not even with Lydia, whom Stacy had once thought Cord might marry, had she ever wanted to start a spitting, hair-pulling fight. It was crazy, because she had despised Lydia while she actually liked Paula. But not with Cord—never with Cord!

Three steps backward into the hallway, she heard Cord speak and stopped to listen, despising herself for listening.

"You could make a fortune with your hands, Paula," he murmured in a husky, caressing voice that had so often quickened Stacy's heartbeat and sent flames of desire shooting through her limbs.

Paula! A jealous voice screamed in her head. He had called her Paula!

The physiotherapist's words at the table came back to haunt Stacy—"When you become someone I can like and respect, then you have permission to call me Paula." Would she correct him now? Stacy held her breath, grinding the back of her hand against her teeth.

"I'm not interested in making a fortune," the blonde replied quietly.

There was no correction. A searing pain plunged through Stacy's heart, nearly doubling her in half.

"What do you want?" Cord spoke again. His decidedly interested tone indicated that the question was more than idle curiosity.

"What every woman wants. A satisfying and rewarding career, a home and a man." An instant of silence followed before Paula added, "Not necessarily in that order."

Not Cord. You can't have Cord, Stacy cried silently.

"Are you hard to please?" he mocked.

"Very," Paula agreed in what sounded like a deliberately light tone.

"The man who gets you will have his hands full." His voice was rimmed with amusement.

"But he'll be man enough to handle me." Despite the smiling sound in Paula's answer, it carried an inflection of complete seriousness.

"That sounds like a challenge," Cord chuckled.

"Are you going to pick up the glove?"

Stacy couldn't tell whether Paula was teasing or trying to make her interest in Cord apparent to him. Paula had warned Stacy the day she arrived that she always fell in love with her patients.

Her eyes burned, but they remained dry as Stacy hastily stumbled into the living room. She was afraid to hear anymore. A chilling dread froze her senses to everything but the image of the two semi-clad people in the master bedroom, and the feminine hands that so freely touched Cord's body when he had denied Stacy the right.

Her white teeth bit into the back of her hand as she sank onto the couch. Sightlessly she stared over the rear cushion at the blue sky visible through the glass doors to the veranda. Something inside her shattered, splintering into a thousand pieces. What was it? Her heart?

Deaf and blind to the world around her, Maria repeated her name several times before Stacy realized she was not alone in the room anymore. She turned blankly to the housekeeper.

"What was it you wanted, Maria?" she asked flatly.

"There is a phone call for you."

Stacy resumed her former position.

"Take their name and phone number and tell them I'll call them back. I don't want to talk to anyone right now."

"I will tell them you will call back this afternoon," Maria agreed.

"Not this afternoon. I won't be in this afternoon," Stacy replied in the same emotionless tone.

"You are never at the house anymore," the housekeeper chided in a sadly scolding tone.

"No, I'm never at the house anymore." It seemed to be a pronouncement of her fate.

Stacy roused herself sufficiently to inquire, "Is lunch nearly ready?"

"A *momento* only," Maria answered.

As Maria left the room, Stacy rose from the couch to mechanically go through the motions of washing up for the meal. She felt very much like a robot sitting at the table silently eating the salad of avocado and grapefruit sections coated with a sweet syrup. Her tongue tasted neither sweet nor sour.

Yet it wasn't her silence that drew comment as Paula, dressed in slacks and a top, glanced curiously at the unnaturally silent Josh seated across the table from her.

"You're very quiet this noon, Josh. Are you tired?" she queried lightly.

His small dark head moved in a negative shake, his gaze never leaving his plate.

"You generally always chatter like a chipmunk," Paula teased. "Something terrible must be bothering you."

"I scolded him for going swimming this morning," Stacy explained blandly when Josh remained silent. Her features were stoically void of any expression as she glanced at the blond woman. "I wasn't aware until afterward that you and Cord had been making daily use of the pool for therapy and that Joshua was supervised and not swimming alone as I'd first supposed. My apologies haven't been fully accepted so far."

"I'm sorry, Stacy. I thought you knew," Paula apologized.

"It doesn't matter," Stacy shrugged. "I know now. Has the, er, swimming been useful?"

She glanced up in time to see the brief look exchanged between Cord and Paula, and her stomach somersaulted sickeningly at the intimately private secret the look implied.

"It hasn't done any harm," the therapist replied diffidently.

A shudder of pain quaked through Stacy. "Excuse me," she murmured. "I just remembered Maria told me there was an important telephone message for me. I was supposed to return it immediately."

It was a feeble excuse, but it was the only one she could think of to leave the table in the middle of a meal. Her retreating footsteps were haunted by how many other secret glances they had exchanged when she wasn't looking.

She cursed her vivid imagination, but it was fed by the vague glitter of contentment in Cord's dark eyes and the lack of any bitter cynicism around the edges of his mouth.

Slipping out through the front door, Stacy knew she would never be able to share another meal with them without wondering what silent message was being transmitted. She resolved not to subject herself to that torture.

Over the next few days she began rearranging things. Travis became her link with sanity, and she used him shamelessly as a buffer. Since Paula had arrived she had invited him over several times each week for dinner. Now she scheduled their ranch meetings at lunchtime. If Travis thought her behavior was odd, he took care not to mention it, treating her almost constant demand for his spare time as natural.

The question Stacy kept ignoring was where would it all end? This day-to-day survival couldn't continue forever.

How long could she avoid acknowledging the relationship that was developing beneath her nose between Cord and Paula?

But what was the alternative? Should she confront Cord with her suspicions and make herself look the fool if she was wrong? Or should she accuse Paula and warn her to stay away from Cord?

Sighing dispiritedly, Stacy looped her chestnut hair behind her ears. Her boots continued carrying her toward the house, her troubled brown eyes staring at the ground.

A squeal of childish delight came from the direction of the house followed by a resounding splash of water. Nearing the slight knoll that permitted her a view of the pool area on the west side of the hacienda, Stacy paused. The red-tiled roof gleamed dully against the whitewashed adobe walls.

Two more steps and she could see the swimming pool and its three occupants. Cord's rolling laughter carried across the distance to her ears. Her chest contracted as she tried to remember the last time she had heard him laugh with such happiness. It must have been shortly after his accident when he had been simply glad to be alive.

She could see Paula's blond head in the water near Cord's. When the physiotherapist turned and said something to him, Cord laughed again. Stacy bit her lip until the salty taste of blood was in her mouth. She had not been able to make him laugh like that, but Paula had.

Jealousy scored another blow. The scene of man, woman and child playing in the swimming pool was an ideal picture of a family unit. The picture was wrong because Stacy should have been there to portray the mother, not Paula. Why did they have to look so happy together, she cried silently.

"They look like they're having fun, don't they?" The male voice jerked Stacy's head in its direction, alarm registering in her widened eyes, and in the sudden draining of color from her face. Concern darkened Travis's gaze.

"I didn't mean to startle you," he said.

"I...it's...okay. I...I just didn't hear you walk up."

Stacy fought to regain her composure with limited success. "You're early. I wasn't expecting you until lunch."

Jerkily she started toward the house, anxious to take his attention away from the occupants of the swimming pool. She didn't think she could talk about them with any degree of poise.

"I can't make lunch today. That's why I stopped now on the off chance I would find you." Travis fell in step beside her. "If you aren't busy now, I thought we could go over those grain invoices together and see if we can find the reason for the discrepancy with our records."

"I'm free," Stacy agreed, grateful she would not have the opportunity to dwell on the scene she had witnessed.

Unfortunately the office work didn't prove to be the distraction that she had hoped it would. Somewhere part way through her stack of papers, she forgot to concentrate on what she was doing. Her gaze wandered instead to the window and the driveway beyond the panes. The laughter and voices from the pool area had ended some time ago, yet the sounds echoed endlessly in her mind.

"Stacy, what's wrong?"

Her reaction was in slow motion as she turned to Travis. "What?" she asked blankly, hearing his voice without hearing his question.

His frowning gaze inspected her face. "I said, what's wrong? Why are you crying?"

Stacy lifted a hand to her cheeks, surprised by the moistness she found there. Hurriedly she wiped the tears away, only to feel the rivulets of more tears retracing the paths of the first. In agitation and embarrassment, she rose from her chair, turning her back to Travis.

"Nothing—really." Her voice quivered, revealing her lie, and more tears slipped from her lashes.

There was the scrape of a chair leg as Travis straightened. Stacy knew she hadn't deceived him. She wiped frantically at the tears and tried to laugh. It was a choking sound.

"I don't know what's the matter with me. I'm sorry, Travis," she muffled the words through her hands, trying to still her quivering lips and chin. "You must think I've lost my mind." It was what Stacy was wondering.

"I think something is wrong," he said quietly. "Will it help to talk about it?"

"Yes—no." She slid her hands behind her neck, letting them rest there for an instant. "I'm so mixed up." A sighing sob accompanied her admission. "I'm such a fool, I know, but you saw them out there."

"Cord and Paula?"

"Did you hear him laugh?" Stacy glanced at Travis's handsome features and the wings of silver lacing the temples of his curling black hair. She turned away from his thoughtful gaze. "I wanted to be the one to make him laugh again. It . . . it sounds selfish, doesn't it? Selfish and jealous?''

Again she wiped at the tears on her cheeks. "I am." Her voice was low and defeated. "It's just that they have become so close—so friendly. I know . . . I'm sure they. . . ." Stacy couldn't put her suspicions into words.

Her throat tightened and silent sobs shook her shoulders. Breaking down like this in front of Travis was too humiliating.

His large hands closed over her shoulders and turned her into his chest. The inviting expanse of shirt snapped what little remained of her control, and she buried her face in his shirt and cried. Travis rocked her gently like a child, stroking the silken length of her chestnut hair, highlighted with gold. Over and over again, Stacy sobbed that she was sorry.

"Ssh," Travis soothed. "You've been living on your nerves for too long, bottling everything up inside. This was bound to happen."

"I didn't want it to," Stacy mumbled brokenly.

"That's beside the point now," he smiled gently.

"If only I didn't think that Cord...
Paul...." She shook her head, pressing her lips
together.

"If you think something is going on between Cord and Paula, then you're letting
your imagination away with you," Travis
scolded gently.

"I want to believe that." Desperately she
wanted to believe that.

Travis crooked a finger under her chin and
raised it to smile into her face.

"It's just a matter of time."

The little breath she exhaled was wistful.
Tremulously she curved her lips into a smile,
appreciating his encouraging words and hop-
ing he was right. Uncertainty lingered in her
tear-wet eyes. Tenderly he wiped the tears from
her left cheek, a soothing roughness to his cal-
lused hand.

Blinking, her gaze swung from his roughly
hewn face toward his wrist. Halfway through
the arc, her gaze was stopped. The study door
was opened and a tall figure stood within the
frame. The jubilant light in the jet dark eyes
flamed into menacing rage, piercing Stacy with
their fury.

Her mouth opened incredulously as she
stared at Cord. He was standing upright,

leaning heavily on a horseshoe-shaped walking aid. But he was standing! She wanted to cry for joy, but she couldn't speak.

At the shining change in her expression, Travis glanced over his shoulder, and instantly his hand fell away from her face. There was an instant when he mirrored the same surprise and gladness as Stacy. But Travis noted, too, the chiseled coldness in Cord's patrician features. Stacy was still too overwhelmed by Cord's recovery to notice the sudden tensing of the man standing next to her.

"First it was Colter's wife, now it's mine, is that it, McCrea?" Cord jeered coldly. "Can't you find a woman who doesn't belong to someone else?"

"You've made a mistake, Cord," Travis replied quietly.

Stunned by the violence in Cord's voice, Stacy finally registered in her mind the construction Cord had built out of the situation. Unhurriedly Travis set her away from him.

"The only mistake I made was being fool enough to trust you!" Cord snapped. "Get out of here at once, McCrea!"

Lifting the horseshoe frame that supported him, he set it inches forward into the room, half dragging his legs after it. After several repetitions of the procedure, the doorway was clear.

"It's not at all true what you're thinking, Cord," Stacy protested as he continued to glare savagely at Travis.

"It's all right, Stacy." But she could see Travis was controlling himself with an effort. "I'll leave for now."

"You're damned right you will!" was Cord's growling agreement.

With smooth strides, Travis walked from the room. When the front door had clicked shut, Cord shifted his diamond-black gaze to Stacy. She shivered at the contempt in his expression.

"I was upset," she defended. "Travis was only trying to make me feel better, that's all."

"Do you expect me to believe that?" he jeered.

"It's the truth."

She shook her head helplessly, her gaze running over his erect figure. "Oh, Cord, you're out of that wheelchair! I can't get over it." She moved blindly toward him, wanting to forget the stupid misunderstanding over Travis and rejoice in Cord's recovery. "I—"

"It was meant to be a surprise. Some surprise!" His mouth thinned bitterly.

The darkening fires in his eyes made Stacy realize that he was revisualizing the scene with Travis when he had opened the study door.

"Please, don't let's argue," she pleaded softly.

The tips of her fingers hesitantly touched his hand on the walker. "This is a time to be happy you're on your feet again. How long? When did it happen?" she asked.

Cord shifted his hand away from her touch. "Does it matter?" he mocked. "Tell me, Stacy, how did it feel to have a man's arms around you?"

His rejection of her tentative caress stung. Stacy drew back, tilting her chin forward. He towered above her, aloof and arrogant.

"Tell me how it feels when Paula touches you, rubbing your shoulders and neck?" she challenged.

"That has nothing to do with what we're talking about!" He became angry at her question. "Don't try to justify your unfaithfulness with her."

"Where's the difference?" She stood stiffly in front of him. Her heart kept waiting for his denial, the few words necessary that would tell her she had simply been imagining that something was going on between him and Paula.

But he ignored the question. "I knew you'd become bored with ranch life and being tied down to one place, but I never suspected for one minute that you would seek a diversion in the arms of another man," he declared in disgust.

Stacy flinched uncontrollably, then recovered. "Would you believe me if I told you that Travis and I are only friends?"

"I'm not blind!" The hard line of his mouth crooked cynically. "I saw the two of you embracing when I opened the door!"

"And you believe everything you see? So do I, then! I guess there's nothing more to say, is there?" She sounded quite calm, but her legs were shaking as she started walking toward the door.

"I want Travis off this ranch within the hour," he snapped.

Her hand rested on the doorknob. She turned, meeting the freezing blackness of his gaze. "I'm the one who's running this ranch, Cord, not you," she replied softly to keep her voice from betraying the quaking of her body. "I was the one who hired Travis and I'll be the one to tell him to leave. And I have no intention of doing so."

Without another word, she opened the door and walked into the hall. She could hear Cord cursing under his breath as he tried to follow her, laboriously dragging each leg a step at a time. She trembled at the raging anger she had incited. Quickly she closed the front door and hurried from the house.

CHAPTER NINE

TRAVIS WAS leaning against the fender of the pickup, the crown of his dusty Stetson pushed back on his head. A cigarette was cupped in his hand as he impassively watched Stacy's approach.

"Did you explain?"

His brown eyes ran over her grim expression and the defiant thrust of her chin.

"Cord was too convinced of his own conclusion to listen," Stacy replied stiffly.

"I'm sorry." Travis flipped his cigarette to the ground and then crushed it beneath the heel of his boot.

"Neither of us had done anything to be sorry about," she retorted with a rush of indignant pride.

"I know that." He stared down the winding lane leading through the broken Texas hills to the main road. "But just the same I think Cord was right when he told me to leave. It would probably be best all the way around.

With me out of the picture, he'll be more apt to listen to you.''

"No!" Stacy violently rejected the idea. "Under no circumstances do I want you to leave unless I personally ask you to go."

Shaking his dark head, Travis looked back at her and sighed. "You're only complicating a difficult situation. His jealousy proves that there's nothing going on between him and Paula. You were only imagining it."

A lump entered her throat. "That's where you're wrong," she said tightly.

His mouth tightened grimly in exasperation. "Stacy, you can't still believe it's possible."

"I confronted Cord with it." Tears burned the back of her eyes, and she bent her head so Travis wouldn't see them. "It's the old case of what's sauce for the gander isn't sauce for the goose. It's one thing for Cord to be unfaithful, but it's unforgivable in his eyes that I should be."

Travis frowned, studying her intently. "I don't believe it."

"It's the truth." Swallowing back the tears, Stacy lifted her gaze. "Travis, I want your word that you'll stay."

He hesitated, carefully considering her request. "I'll stay for the time being." His reluctant agreement indicated that he thought she was making a mistake by asking him to remain.

"Thank you," she murmured gratefully. Pausing for a second, she added, "And I'm sorry about the reference Cord made to Natalie."

Travis took a deep breath and stared into space again. "I love her."

His mouth crooked wryly. "I'm afraid I haven't got to the point where I can say it in the past tense. Maybe I never will. But there was never anything physical between us. She was always Colter's. She was never mine to take. They're happy now and I couldn't wish any more than that."

Abruptly he turned and walked to the driver's door of the pickup. "Since I'm still on the payroll, I'd better get to work."

Stacy didn't attempt to stop him. "I'll see you later, Travis, and thanks—for everything."

When she returned to the house at lunchtime, Stacy expected another confrontation with Cord, but there was nothing but glacial silence as they faced each other over the table.

Before the meal was over, she wished there had been a volcanic eruption instead.

His chilling attitude didn't change one degree during the next three days, and Stacy didn't make any attempt to begin a thaw. She had tried to explain once and Cord wouldn't listen. She was too stubborn and proud to try again.

Cross-legged on the end of the bed, she methodically brushed her long hair, electricity crackling through the silken strands.

Once she had thought things couldn't get any worse between herself and Cord. How very wrong she had been!

There was a light rap on her bedroom door, and she tensed, her heart quickening with hope.

"Who is it?" She hadn't heard the labored sounds of Cord's footsteps, but the carpet might have muffled them.

"It's me, Paula. May I come in?"

"Come in." It seemed almost like admitting a traitor into the camp. As the door opened, Stacy resumed the rhythmic strokes of the brush through her hair, not glancing up. "What was it you wanted, Paula?" she asked briskly.

"I hoped you weren't in bed yet. There was something I wanted to talk to you about." There was no indication that Paula had noticed the absence of welcome in Stacy's voice.

"What is it?" Deliberately she didn't suggest that the physiotherapist take a seat in the velvet-covered chair in the corner.

"It's about Cord."

Paula didn't wait for an invitation and settled her tall frame on the chair.

"Yes?" Stacy prompted coolly.

"Lately he's reverted to his old snarling self."

Uncurling her legs from beneath her, Stacy walked to the vanity table and stood in front of the mirror.

"So I've noticed," she responded indifferently. Actually Cord hadn't spoken a word to her, but she heard him snapping at everyone else.

"In a way, I expected it," Paula said.

She rose from the chair and moved to join her reflection with Stacy's in the mirror. "He's on his feet again and replaced the walker with crutches, but he's not as mobile yet as he wants to be. When I first came here, I had to bully him into the therapy. Now he's trying too hard."

"I see," Stacy murmured, but she kept all of her attention focused on fluffing her hair into its style.

"If I don't find some way to distract him, he'll overdo it."

There was a second's pause as Paula waited for Stacy's comment, but she made none. She sensed that the therapist had a suggestion to make and she, in turn, waited for it. "There's no reason why he can't begin taking part in the operation of the ranch. I want you to talk to him about it."

"No!" The word exploded from Stacy as her flashing gaze swung to Paula's reflection. She wouldn't seek Cord out for any reason. Placing the hairbrush on the table, she moved toward the window. "It wouldn't do any good. Travis and I have tried many times before."

"You have to try again," Paula declared quietly but firmly.

"He—he wouldn't listen to me," Stacy argued. "You would be much better off to suggest it to him yourself."

"He might not listen to you, not if—" Paula conceded, qualifying the admission with "—he still thought you really didn't need his help and were trying to patronize him. But anyone taking a look at you, Stacy, would realize that you're overworked. All you have to do is plead that you can't cope with all of it anymore. It's unarguable fact."

Stacy had seen her reflection in the mirror. Blue shadow rimmed her eyes, eyes that had become a dull, flat brown except when she was roused to anger. The hollows of her cheeks accented her bones and hardly a glimmer of happiness remained in her features. Even the gold-dust sprinkle of freckles across her nose lacked the usual appeal.

Although Paula's words were valid, Stacy couldn't bring herself to agree, and she felt mean to refuse, so she made no reply.

"Stacy, what's the matter with you?" Paula demanded. "You almost act as if you don't want Cord to recover completely."

"That's not true!" she denied, spinning to face the tall blonde.

"Something has happened between you and Cord, hasn't it?" Blue eyes watched Stacy alertly. "What is it?"

Stacy turned away from the scrutiny. "You'll have to ask Cord," she answered stiffly.

"I have. He told me to mind my own business."

"Then that's my answer, too."

"I won't accept that from you," Paula responded. "I don't care whether you think I'm sticking my nose in where it doesn't belong or not. My concern is Cord and what's best for him. I thought that was your only concern, too, regardless of any petty misunderstanding."

Staring at her twisting fingers, Stacy cried inwardly at the unfairness of being blackmailed by her love.

"I am concerned." Her voice was barely above a whisper.

"If you are, then talk to him," the blonde challenged. "Persuade him to take some of the work off your shoulders. Give him something to do other than brood all day long."

"All . . . all right."

The reluctant agreement was released through gritted teeth as Stacy brushed a hand across her temple and gazed sightlessly at the ceiling. "I'll talk to him tomorrow," she frowned.

"Tonight," Paula said unequivocally. "Putting it off until tomorrow won't make it any easier."

Stacy pivoted, meeting the directness of the blue gaze. The angry protest rising in her throat was checked by her tightly compressed lips. Without a word, she swept past the tall blonde through the door and down the stairs to the master bedroom.

There her own courage faltered. She stared at the closed door for a hesitating second, her hand clenching nervously. Quickly she rapped once and opened the door without waiting for permission to enter. Cord was standing freely at the end of the bed, a hand clutching the sturdy post of the Spanish style bed. His expression was grim with determination as he glanced up. At the sight of Stacy, he drew his dark head back in aloof arrogance.

"What do you want?" he challenged.

Skirting his cold gaze, Stacy glanced at his crutches some distance away. "What are you doing?" she breathed, alarm surfacing at the obvious unsteadiness of his legs.

Half dragging and half lifting one leg forward to put himself at a better angle to face her, Cord lifted one corner of his mouth.

"Don't you recognize the movement?" he mocked cynically. "It's my version of walking."

"But you could fall," she protested, realizing what Paula had been talking about. Cord was trying to push himself beyond the limit of his capabilities at this moment.

He leaned a hip against the bed railing. She could see by the rippling muscles in his arms the effort was costing him to remain upright. He was clad only in dark trousers, his shirt discarded. Perspiration curled the dark hairs on his naked chest.

"I'm not interested in listening to your false gestures of concern," he jeered. "Get to the point of why you're here. I know it's not a desire for my company that's brought you."

Stacy's mouth opened to deny his cutting remark, but she closed it without speaking. It would be a waste of breath. He wouldn't believe her.

"I need your help," she said finally.

A black eyebrow arched in arrogant disbelief. "For what?"

"The ranch work has become too much for me. I can't handle it all anymore," Stacy rushed.

There was more than a grain of truth in the statement. Managing the ranch was a full-time occupation without the added burden of the coming horse sale.

"What's the matter?" Cord mocked harshly. "Don't you have enough free time to sneak off to meet Travis? Are you expecting me to provide it?"

Stacy flinched at the physical blow to his sarcasm. In agitation she moved with no direction to her steps, a release of the frustration and pain that consumed her.

"Travis has nothing to do with my request in any way," she denied in a low, trembling voice.

"Doesn't he?" Cord snarled.

His sunbrowned fingers closed savagely around her wrist and yanked her to him. The force of the sudden contact with his hard male shape momentarily took her breath away. Her wrist was released as his hand gathered a handful of her gleaming hair and viciously twisted it to pull her head back. Stacy gasped, wincing at the pain her scalp.

Her eyes opened to focus on the glittering fire in his gaze. The thud of her heart sounded like a hammer pounding her chest. His gaze centered on the parted moistness of her lips.

"Is Travis a good lover, my passionate Stacy?" he hissed.

His gaze traveled downward to the exposed curve of her neck. "Do you make those kitten sounds in your throat for him?"

Relentlessly he bruised the sensitive cord of her neck as if intent on destroying any trace of

another man's caress. He paused near her ear
to nibble cruelly at its lobe.

Hot fire raced through Stacy's veins, melt-
ing her bones. Her fingers spread over the hard
flesh of his shoulders, muscles bunched and
flexing beneath her palms. The scent of his
body was musky and warm, arousing her
senses with familiar desire. But it was not desire driving Cord, only a ruthlessness to claim
what was his.

"Don't do this, Cord. Please," Stacy
begged.

Her protest was instantly smothered by the
grinding force of his mouth. Yielding against
him, she knew she couldn't deny him his way.
The bitter truth was that she wanted his ca-
resses even if they were prompted by anger and
contempt.

As she leaned against him, his knees buckled. He was forced to release her to let his arms
grip the bed, taking the bulk of his weight
away from his still weak legs. Instantly Stacy
reached forward when she realized what had
happened, anxious to lend him her support.

"Let me help you," she said.

Cord turned away from her, struggling to
keep his balance. "I don't want your help!" he
hurled savagely. "Just get out of here!"

Biting into her lower lip, swollen from the cruel mastery of his kiss, Stacy took a step backward. Then she turned and hurried blindly toward the door.

His voice snarled after her. "And you can tell your precious Travis that you weren't able to trick your husband into allowing you more time for your rendezvous!"

Stacy stopped at the door. "For the last time, Cord, Travis had nothing to do with my coming here." Her voice quivered with pain. "The quarter-horse auction is only a week away. I can't cope with everything there is to do."

She made one last attempt to fulfill the purpose that had brought her to the room. "I talked to Paula and she said that your helping with the ranch probably wouldn't interfere with the therapy."

Her back was turned to him as she reached for the doorknob. It turned beneath her hand before he replied to her statement.

"When did you talk to Paula?" he demanded quietly.

A frown marred her forehead. "A few minutes ago. She's upstairs."

She released the doorknob and faced him. "What difference does that make?"

"Was this her idea or yours?" His gaze narrowed.

"It was Paula's idea," she answered truthfully. "But it doesn't change the fact that I need help, Cord, your help. I once said I would ask for no quarter from you, but now I'm begging for it. I can't make it without you." Stacy meant that in every sense of the word, but she qualified it almost instantly out of pride. "At least, you could do the bookwork if nothing else."

He seemed to weigh her appeal, testing its sincerity, then nodded grudgingly. "I'll do the bookwork. Now go away and leave me alone."

He began the slow task of walking beside the bed, his arms bearing most of the burden as he made it clear the dismissal was final.

Knowing any offer of assistance would be summarily rejected, Stacy left the room. Listlessly she climbed the stairs, walking past her room to Paula's. The door was opened and she paused in its frame.

"Cord has agreed to help," she said simply.

"I knew you could persuade him," Paula smiled.

One corner of Stacy's mouth lifted in a bitter movement. She felt that Paula's name had lent more weight with Cord than her own plea for aid. She made no reply to the comment as she turned and retreated to the emptiness of her bedroom. Her body was haunted by the memory of Cord's. There would be no rest tonight. Nor the next two nights.

WEARILY SHE pushed the front door open, wondering why she had bothered to come to the house for lunch. She was too tired to eat and felt as brittle as an eggshell.

There was a rustling of papers from the study. The door stood open and Stacy guessed that Cord was in the room working. She started to hurry silently by, not wanting to see him when she was so vulnerable to his barbs.

"Stacy! Come in here!"

His imperious order checked her in midstride. She hesitated, then moved into the doorway. He was sitting behind the desk, his patrician features darkened in anger.

"What do you want?" Her brisk question was intended to imply that she was busy and impatient to be on her way.

"I want an explanation for this." Lifting his hand to indicate the papers he held, he tossed them to the front of the desk for her inspection.

Stacy paused, wanting to flee. Resolutely squaring her shoulders, she walked to the desk and picked up the papers. A quick glance identified them as the catalog of the yearlings to be sold.

"What do you want explained?" she frowned, seeing nothing that was in error.

"Why are two stud colts sired by Lije Masters' stallion listed for sale?" he demanded.

Stacy shrugged her shoulders in confusion. "Neither Travis nor I saw any reason to keep them. We already have three two-year-old stallions for stud prospects as well as the proven stallion you bought last year. That's not even mentioning the two we already use for breeding."

His mouth tightened grimly. "You knew I wanted to add the Malpais bloodline to my stock. This one yearling out of the Cutters' mare I especially wanted to keep."

"How in the world could I know that?" Stacy protested angrily. "Am I supposed to read your mind?"

"You could have used some common sense," he retorted.

"I asked you to help choose the yearlings to sell!" she shouted in defense, her raw nerves unable to tolerate his anger. "Travis told you he didn't know anything about horses, only cattle. You refused to help, so don't blame me if there are horses listed that you don't want to sell. It's your own fault."

"How was I supposed to know you would do something as stupid as this?" Cord waved angrily at the catalog.

Hot tears spilled over her lashes, flaming her cheeks with their scalding warmth.

"I can't do anything to please you anymore!" she declared in a choked voice. "If you think I'm doing such a lousy job of running things, then you can do it all from now on! I'm handing in my resignation as of this moment!"

Pivoting, she raced from the room, half-blinded by her tears. A hand covered her mouth to stifle the sobs that wrenched her throat.

"Stacy, come back here!" Cord shouted.

She slammed the front door on his order. Her headlong flight took her down the sloping grade to the stables. Throwing open the door to the tack room, she pulled a bridle from the wall and her saddle and blanket. Indifferent to the weight, she walked swiftly to the corral, but there was no sign of the chocolate-brown mare.

From a sturdy enclosure apart from the others came a whinny of greeting. Stacy glanced in its direction, her gaze focusing on the sorrel stallion. His delicate head was over the top rail, luminous brown eyes returning her look, pointed ears pricked forward.

"Diablo," Stacy murmured with decision, and moved to his corral.

Docilely the red horse nuzzled her arm, playfully nipping at her blouse as she entered his corral. He bent his head without argument to accept the bridle, and swished his flaxen tail contentedly as she laid the saddle blanket on his back.

Minutes later Stacy was swinging into the saddle, mentally thumbing her nose at Cord's long-standing order not to ride the high-spirited stallion. With her weight on his back, the sorrel pranced eagerly. His four white feet stirred up the dusty ground.

Running a soothing hand over his arched neck, Stacy turned him toward the corral gate. From the corner of her eye, she saw the wizened figure hurrying to intercept them. She leaned forward and unlatched the gate only to have Hank reach it before she could swing it open.

"You get down off that horse!" He held the gate shut as he frowned at her, certain she had lost all her senses.

"Get out of the way, Hank," she ordered.

"You know you ain't supposed to ride that stallion."

"He's my horse and I'll do what I want."

Stacy nudged the sorrel forward until his shoulder was pushing against the gate. Her hand joined the effort to swing the gate open. "Move, Hank," she warned.

"The boss gave strict orders none of us was to let you ride that horse!" He strained to keep it closed, but the combined strength of horse and rider was more than he could stop, especially when the sorrel saw the narrow opening and pushed to enlarge it.

"I don't care what the boss says!" Stacy declared.

Hank was knocked to the ground as the horse burst through. Stacy had only a second to glance back to make certain the old man was getting to his feet unharmed. After that, all her efforts were directed to controlling her mount.

Reining him away from the fenced enclosures of the other horses, she guided him toward the house and the winding lane that would take them to open range. In a lunging canter, the sorrel threatened to bolt with each stride. The leather reins bit into her hands as she tried to hold him.

Cord was on the sidewalk when the stallion plunged by the house. One look at Stacy fighting to hold the horse and he began shouting orders to the stable hands emerging from the buildings. A smile curved her mouth, guessing his anger at seeing her astride the horse he had forbidden her to ride.

Her pleasure was short-lived. She had to concentrate on mastering the spirited steed beneath her. It had been so long since Diablo had tasted freedom and he wanted to drink his fill. Lack of sleep and loss of weight had depleted Stacy's strength, and the muscles in her arms began to tremble at the effort of holding the stallion in a controllable canter.

With a determined shake of his head, the sorrel loosened the hold on the reins and gained the bit between his teeth. In one bound, he was at a dead run, breaking away from the driveway to veer across the rolling plains racing toward the eastern mountains.

The wind whipped Stacy's breath away. A blackness swam around her eyes as she buried her face in the flaxen mane and gripped the saddle horn to stay on. Dodging patches of prickly pear cactus and skimming over the top of sagebrush and range grass, the stallion ran with ecstasy.

Somehow Stacy managed to stay in the saddle, aboard the runaway, mindless to the wild ride. Not until he slowed to a bone-jarring trot miles from the ranch house did she take notice of her surroundings. His flanks heaved as he blew the dust from his lungs and finally obeyed the pressure of the reins when she drew him to a stop.

Weakly, she slipped from the saddle, a death grip remaining on the reins. Her knees buckled beneath her and she slumped to the ground. Diablo was content to munch the long strands of grass. For the moment Stacy didn't care if he broke away. She lay there on the ground, strength gradually flowing back into her limbs.

But it was nearly an hour before she climbed back into the saddle and turned the horse toward home.

CHAPTER TEN

BOTH STACY and Diablo were hot and tired by the time they gained sight of the ranch yard. Pausing beside the wrought-iron fence enclosing the family cemetery on a knoll west of the house, Stacy indifferently watched the activity below. The circuitous route she had taken had been necessary in order to get her bearing after the wild ride.

Travis's green pickup truck was parked in the driveway in front of the house. The door to the driver's side was opened. The broad-shouldered figure sitting half in the cab and half out was undoubtedly Travis.

There was also no mistaking the identity of Cord leaning on his crutches and gazing in the direction Stacy had originally gone. Paula was there, too, her hands on her hips conveying an attitude of troubled concern.

A search party had obviously been organized for her. Stacy guessed that Travis was probably in contact with it now, via the radio in the truck. She supposed she hadn't run into it because of the different route she had taken back.

Touching a heel to the sorrel, she started down the small hill toward the truck. There was no thought to Cord's anger at her deliberate disobedience that would await her return. She seemed invulnerable to everything but her own tiredness.

She was a hundred feet away before Travis glanced around and noticed her approach. He stepped quickly out of the truck, saying something to the other two. With a jerk of his head, Cord looked at her, a taut alertness about him like a lion ready to spring.

It was Travis who moved forward to intercept her, his hand grasping the reins near the cheek strap. Diablo tossed his head, disliking the touch of a man's hand.

Travis ignored the stallion, his gaze sweeping over Stacy's disheveled appearance. Dirt clung to the shoulder and sleeve of her blouse where she had rested on the ground.

"Are you all right, Stacy?"

"Yes," she smiled wanly.

Looping the reins around the saddle horn, she swung her right leg over the horn, kicking her other foot free of the stirrup to slide to the ground. But Travis's hands were around her waist, lifting her down. For a brief instant she stumbled against him before regaining her balance.

Almost absently her gaze met the blaze of Cord's dark eyes, blistering hotly over her. She stepped away from Travis's supporting hands.

"Get that stallion out of here, Travis," ordered Cord. "And as for you, Stacy—" His voice was ominously low.

Paula placed a restraining hand on his arm. "Let her be, Cord," she murmured. Her blue eyes moved sympathetically to Stacy's exhausted expression. "She's hot and tired. She needs a shower and a rest, not a lecture."

A muscle worked convulsively in Cord's jaw as if he wasn't entirely convinced of Paula's statement. Before he could complete his interrupted sentence, Paula walked around him and curved an arm around Stacy's shoulders, turning her toward the house. "Come on, Stacy."

In other circumstances, Stacy would have resented the other girl's proprietorial air. At the moment she was too tired to care. It didn't even matter that she had been rescued from Cord's wrath. She was numbed beyond emotion.

The sting of the shower spray eliminated that protection. Wrapped in a cotton robe, Stacy stood at her bedroom window watching the search party that had just ridden in, recalled by either Cord or Travis. Guilt nagged her at the amount of work undone because they had searched for her. Riding Diablo had been a childish gesture of defiance.

A peculiar thudding sound came from the staircase, and Stacy tipped her head in absent curiosity. It stopped outside her door, and a wave of certainty washed over her that it was Cord outside. A second later the door opened to reveal him, anger darkening his face with a thundercloud warning.

"Did you think by staying in your room you would avoid facing me?" he challenged.

She shook her head without verbally answering and stared out the window. A whole gamut of painful sensations returned.

"You deliberately rode that horse knowing how I felt, didn't you?" His harshly condemning voice scraped at her barely healed nerves.

"Yes," she admitted quietly.

"You realize you could have been very seriously hurt, don't you? And don't pretend that you had control of that horse, because he was running away with you.''

"But I wasn't hurt," she defended with forced evenness.

"That's beside the point," Cord snapped.

Irritatedly she swung away from the window. "There's no reason to go into all this. It's over and done with and I admit it was foolish. I was . . . I was just upset."

"You're right," he said tightly. "It is over and done with. And it won't happen again. Diablo will be off this ranch before nightfall."

It was a full second before his statement penetrated. "What do you mean?" Stacy demanded.

"I'm selling him," declared Cord flatly. "Never again am I going through what I did this afternoon."

"He's not yours to sell!" Temper flashed in her brown eyes. "Diablo belongs to me!"

There was a complacent curve to his firm mouth. "The ranch belongs to me—you even handed the running of it over to me this morning. And I refuse to have that stallion on my property. You can fight the sale, but you can't fight that."

"How can you do this?" Her chin quivered with anger.

"How could you do what you did?" he countered.

"I told you I was upset!"

"And I'm insuring that the next time you're upset, you don't go riding off and breaking your foolish neck!"

"You can't sell him. He's mine," Stacy repeated.

"He'll not stay another night on this ranch," Cord reiterated just as forcefully as Stacy.

"If he goes, I leave with him!" she threatened.

To add credibility to her words, she pivoted away from Cord with a defiant flourish, but before she could take a step, his hand encircled her wrist and spun her back.

"You are not leaving here!" Cruelly he gripped her wrist.

Needing a hand on a crutch to remain upright, there wasn't any way Cord could check the open palm of Stacy's free hand as it swung toward his cheek. It stuck its mark, his tanned skin marked with white then filled with red. For a cold instant, she thought he was going to retaliate in kind.

Stone-faced, Cord released her hand and maneuvered himself in awkward steps to the hall door. There he paused, the glowing dark coals of his eyes seeking her.

"I'm not letting you go, so don't try." It wasn't a warning. It was an unequivocal statement.

As the door closed behind him, Stacy slumped on to her bed, rubbing her bruised wrist.

After several minutes she went to the bedroom window and waited to see if Cord was really going to get rid of Diablo.

If he did, she wasn't certain what she would do. She was afraid that temper had brought them both to an impasse and pride wouldn't allow either of them to back down.

There was no activity in the driveway below, no movement of horse trailers or vans. Perhaps Cord had reconsidered, she thought hopefully.

Then an almost imperceptible click of the doorknob turned her head. Very slowly the door swung partially open. Stacy watched it warily. Josh peered around the door.

His round dark eyes found her and he asked, "Are you sick, mommy?"

"No, I'm not sick," she smiled with loving indulgence. "Come in."

Still he hesitated. "Maria said I wasn't to bother you and I thought you were sick."

"I was just very tired and thought I would rest for a while," Stacy explained more fully to her doubting son.

"Are you all rested now?" Josh inquired, stepping just inside the door. His expression was expectantly bright.

She inclined her head towards him in amusement. "Why?"

"Cause," he shrugged, "I got nothing to do. I thought you might think of something."

Gazing at the hopeful light in his nearly black eyes, Stacy knew she had spent little time with her son lately. There wasn't any reason not to make up for it now.

"Any suggestions in particular that you wanted me to make?" she teased.

An impish smile curved his mouth. "We could play ball."

"How about something less strenuous like swinging?" she suggested.

"Okay," Josh agreed readily.

"Give me five minutes to get dressed and I'll be down," Stacy promised.

With a nod of his head, he darted into the hall. She wasted no time changing into a pair of shorts and a cool top.

At the door, she glanced to the bedroom window, then walked out. There would be plenty of time to find out what Cord was doing about Diablo. She didn't mind postponing her own decision.

It was a carefree afternoon Stacy spent playing with Josh, pushing his swing high in the air and listening to his shrieks of delight. She ruffled the top of Josh's head affectionately as they approached the house.

"Why don't you see if Maria has anything cold to drink?" said Stacy.

"And cookies?" Josh added.

"And cookies," she agreed. "We'll have it out here on the veranda. You can help Maria carry it out, can't you?"

"Sure."

He dashed toward the sliding glass doors as Stacy settled contentedly on a chaise longue. The glass door wasn't completely closed by Josh, and with a sigh at his impatience, Stacy rose to close it.

The loud impact of something falling stopped her hand from sliding the door shut. Identifying the location of the sound as the study, she pushed the door open and darted inside. Her heart kept skipping beats at the thought that Cord might have fallen.

She was not alone in her fear as she spied Paula already racing from the living room toward the study. The physiotherapist's haste lent wings to Stacy's feet. She followed the girl with no hope of reaching Cord first. As she entered the hallway, Paula disappeared through the study door.

"You crazy, idiotic darling!" Stacy heard Paula exclaim in mock reproof. "What on earth were you trying to do?"

The unconsciously murmured endearment slowed Stacy's feet.

A cold chill ran through her veins, reducing her pulse to a dull thud.

"I was trying to get some papers from the file." Cord muttered his answer. His voice was low and strained as if from physical effort.

"Yes, you were trying to get them without your crutches," Paula reprimanded. "When are you going to learn that you have to take things by stages? You'll walk soon enough if you don't break a leg first. Are you hurt anywhere?"

Stacy paused near the door, giving herself a limited angle to view the room. Jealously she watched the tall blonde kneel beside Cord, the contrast between his dark looks and Paula's fairness crushing the life from her heart.

"I think I'm only suffering from a gravely wounded pride," he answered, levering himself into a half-sitting position with one arm and struggling to persuade his uncoordinated legs to shift him to his feet.

"Let me help you," Paula stated.

Without waiting for his agreement, she hooked his arm around her neck and shoulders. The physical effort of both of them brought Cord upright, and he wavered unsteadily for a few seconds, trying to regain his balance.

Razor-sharp claws sliced at Stacy's heart. Paula's height brought the top of her head even with Cord's dark eyes. The fullness of her lips was just below the jutting angle of his chin.

They stood so closely together with Cord's arm around her shoulders that tears of impotent rage welled in Stacy's eyes. When the grooves around his mouth deepened and Cord looked so warmly into the pair of blue eyes, Stacy held her breath to keep from crying out in pain.

"You're one in a million, Paula," he said.

"I'm glad you finally recognize that," she responded lightly,

"Oh, I've recognized it for a long time," Cord nodded.

The half-smile deepened the corners of his mouth. "I just haven't got around to saying anything until now."

Paula's ash-blond head moved downward as if glancing at the floor. Stacy knew the impact of Cord's charm, especially at such close quarters. Cord placed a thumb and forefinger beneath Paula's chin and turned her face toward him again.

"Do you know something?" he asked rhetorically. "I don't think I'll throw you out of the house when all this is finished."

"Careful," Paula warned huskily, "or I might make you live up to that statement."

Cord shook his head and smiled. "You're welcome to stay in my home for as long as you want."

Paula seemed to catch her breath, then laughed with brittle lightness. "Stacy might have something to say about another woman taking up residence here," she reminded him.

His handsome, patrician features immediately hardened, the line of his mouth straightening. A guardedly aloof look entered his gaze as he released Paula's chin.

"Yes," he agreed quietly, "if Stacy is still here."

Reeling away from the study door, Stacy stumbled back toward the veranda. Jumbled thoughts whirled through her head. His enigmatic statement echoed and reechoed in her mind, its meaning no clearer than when he had spoken it. The only certainty in it was that Cord considered it a distinct possibility that she, Stacy, would be gone. The question unanswered was would she leave at her instigation or his?

For two days, Stacy wandered aimlessly through each waking hour, waiting in dread for the death blow to fall. Diablo was still in his corral. She hadn't the courage to ask Cord if he had reconsidered his threat to sell the horse. She feared the result of such a confrontation.

The entire ranch was bustling with preparations for the quarter-horse auction on Saturday, only two days away. Only Stacy and Paula had nothing to do. Stacy's nerves couldn't tolerate the company of the woman who was stealing Cord's love as she restored his mobility.

The lovely old hacienda with its whitewashed adobe and red-tiled roof became a stifling prison, which she had to escape from for some part of each day. The shopping expedition that had brought Stacy into McCloud, Texas, had merely been an excuse to flee from the sword-of-Damocles atmosphere of the house.

Josh tugged at her hand. "I'm hungry, mommy," he said.

Catching back a sigh, Stacy glanced at her watch. It was nearly time for lunch. She knew Maria was expecting them back, but she had no desire to return yet.

"Why don't we have something to eat here in town instead of going home?" she suggested with forced brightness.

"Yeah!" he agreed with a wide grin.

As they entered the restaurant, one familiar face stood out from the others of the townspeople. Josh saw him at the moment Stacy did.

"Look mom, there's Travis!" His loud voice turned heads, including the foreman's.

Travis straightened from the table as Josh withdrew his hand from Stacy's and rushed forward to greet him. She would rather have avoided the discerning pair of brown eyes, but she followed her son.

"Hello, Josh." Travis playfully mussed the shining black hair of her son's head before lifting his gaze to Stacy, its look faintly probing. "Stacy," he nodded a greeting.

"Hello, Travis," she returned with a voice that she hoped sounded calm. "We didn't expect to see you in here."

"I had an errand in town and thought I'd have something to eat before going back. Would you care to join me?" He gestured toward the empty chairs at his table.

It would have been churlish to refuse. "Of course," she accepted with inner reluctance.

Travis had already ordered before they arrived. After the waitress had taken hers and Josh's order, Stacy fiddled nervously with the cutlery until she felt Travis watching the movement. Quickly she hid her hands in her lap and tried to fill the silence that had gaped alarmingly.

"How are things at the ranch?"

It seemed a strange question to ask, yet Stacy had had no contact with the operation of the ranch for nearly a week.

"Running smoothly," Travis replied. "Cord has taken charge as if he'd never been away."

"That's good," she nodded stiffly. Hesitating, she asked, "Has he said anymore about you—leaving?"

"Not directly." He lifted the coffee mug and held it in two hands, swirling the brown black liquid. "He said he needed my legs for the time being."

"I'm sorry for not warning you in advance that I was turning things over to him." Stacy glanced self-consciously at the table top.

"I guessed it was a sudden decision." Travis sipped the coffee. "How is it going with you two?"

"We haven't talked much." That was an understatement. "Before I was busy with the ranch. Now, Cord is."

She watched Josh flipping through the pages of the coloring book she had bought him, as she avoided the introspective gaze of the man seated opposite her. "And he still has to spend a lot of time with Paula," she added.

"You don't still believe—" The waitress arrived, interrupting Travis's impatient comment.

The arrival of the meal brought Josh's attention back to the table and Travis wasn't able to reintroduce the subject, to Stacy's relief.

Her son's chatter covered her own lack of participation in the subsequent conversation.

"Are you going to the ranch now, Travis?" Josh wanted to know as the three of them paused outside the restaurant.

Travis adjusted his dust-stained Stetson on his dark head and nodded affirmatively. "I have to go back to work."

"We're going back now, too," Josh said with certainty.

Stacy couldn't argue with his statement. They had exhausted the morning wandering through stores, and Josh's interest in the outing was over. She couldn't expect her son to understand that she wasn't eager to return to the ranch. It was his home, even if she had begun to feel uncomfortable in it.

"Where is your car parked?" Travis glanced at Stacy.

"Over by the lumber yard." She motioned in the general direction of its location.

"So is my truck." He winked at Josh. "How about a piggyback ride to your car, Josh?" At the boy's eager nod, Travis hoisted him onto his shoulders. "Watch the hat," he warned Josh's clasping hands, "and my neck."

With Josh giggling, Travis started walking toward the lumber yard. His large hands firmly held the small legs dangling across his chest.

"Giddy-up, horsey!" Josh laughed, moving back and forth across the shoulders to urge Travis to go faster.

"Careful or I'll buck you off." Travis tipped his head back in a mock threat.

Stacy laughed at the wide-eyed look on Josh's face as his hands tightly clutched the strong neck for a second before he realized that Travis was only teasing. As they were about to step off the sidewalk curb into the street, a small lime-green car slowed to a stop in front of them, blocking their path.

In disbelief, Stacy stared into the impenetrable mask of coldness that was Cord's face. He was sitting in the passenger seat, his tall frame looking cramped in the close quarters of the economy car. His unrevealing gaze was narrowed on the man carrying his son.

"I thought you were at the ranch, Travis," he said flatly.

"I had an errand in town," was the calm reply as Travis swung Josh down from his perch.

Stacy silently marveled at the way Travis ignored the underlying accusation in Cord's statement. The ruthless set of Cord's jaw made her shiver, yet nothing seemed to ruffle Travis, a trait he had probably gained through years of working for Colter Langston.

Her thoughts were jerked back to the present as Cord's gaze sliced from Travis to her with condemning force, silently accusing her of keeping an assignation with the foreman.

"Josh and I ran into Travis at the restaurant when we stopped for lunch," she explained, hating herself immediately for explaining why she was in Travis's company.

In the driver's seat, Paula bent her head to look past Cord at the threesome standing on the sidewalk. "You were in town shopping, weren't you, Stacy?" she asked.

"Yes," she agreed quickly.

"What did you buy?" Cord glanced pointedly at the thin paper bag in her hand.

Stacy's fingers tightened on it instinctively. "A coloring book for Josh."

"And you've been gone all morning?" Cord mocked.

"I—I couldn't find anything else I wanted," she defended weakly, knowing she hadn't looked at anything but in the most abstract way.

"After spending such a futile morning, it was fortunate you accidentally ran into Travis and weren't forced to eat lunch alone."

An undercurrent of sarcasm and contempt laced Cord's low voice.

"Yes, it was," Stacy agreed, shaking back her head in a gesture of pride and sending her chestnut hair dancing around her shoulders. Her defense was shaky, so she tried to attack. "If I had known you and Paula were going to be in town, I would have met you for lunch."

"It was time for Cord's checkup," Paula explained. "And Bill was too busy to get away to come to the ranch."

"Then you haven't eaten," Stacy commented, glad the image of the two of them sharing an intimate lunch could be banished from her mind.

"Actually Mary talked us into eating with them," she said.

A fingernail broke through the thin paper bag as Stacy tightly clenched it in her hand. Now Paula was even usurping her position with Mary, one of her best friends. The thought choked her.

"I see," she responded, tautly soft.

"We're on our way back to the ranch now," Paula inserted.

"So are we." Stacy coupled herself with Travis in deliberate defiance, uncaring of the diamond sharp look from Cord.

"We'll see you there." Shifting the car into gear, Paula lifted a hand in goodbye, which Stacy managed to stiffly return.

With their way across the street cleared, Stacy took hold of Josh's hand. As they stepped off, Travis lingered for an instant on the curb staring after the car. Then he fell in beside them.

"When Cord gets an idea in his head, he doesn't let go," he said.

Stacy knew he was referring to Cord's belief that she and Travis were having an affair, but she didn't comment. There wasn't anything to say.

CHAPTER ELEVEN

THERE WAS a tired movement of her mouth into a smile. The shining dark head on the white pillow looked so peaceful and happy. Long, curling lashes lay softly against Josh's tanned cheeks. He had been so adamantly opposed to the suggestion of a nap, yet he had fallen asleep before she had reached the last page of the storybook.

Quietly she closed the door to his room. She thought how blissful it could be to have the innocent, untroubled sleep of a child for one night. But then there were occasions when they had nightmares, too.

Halfway down the stairs, Stacy heard the thump of Cord's crutches in the hallway below. Freezing for an instant at the sound, she was motionless when Cord's frowning countenance glanced at her.

"Do you know where Travis is?" he demanded curtly.

"No." She started down the stairs.

"I thought you kept track of him," Cord mocked.

"You think a lot of things that are wrong," she retorted.

"You're all sweetness and innocence, aren't you?" His mouth quirked.

"Just as much as you are," Stacy flashed.

"What's that supposed to mean?" he glowered.

"You figure it out." Impatient that she had allowed herself to become involved in a meaningful trade of innuendoes, she started to walk past him to the living room.

"Don't walk away from me!" Cord snapped, grabbing her arm and spinning her back.

Stacy's temper flared. "Of course not! That's unthinkable! I'm one of your possessions, am I not? Do you keep me around for decoration or for the sake of appearances?" she challenged hoarsely.

"It certainly isn't for decoration!" His gaze raked her thinning figure with scorn. "I can feel your bones beneath my hands. You're turning into a scarecrow, wasting away."

His contempt of her appearance hurt. "Dying for love from you." The words were torn from her throat before she could check them.

"Pining for your freedom is more like it." Cord dismissed her truthful admission with disdain. The crutches beneath his arms supported him as his fingers dug into the soft flesh of her upper arms, and gave her a violent shake.

"Isn't it? Admit it, Stacy. You want to be free, don't you?"

Free from what, her whirling mind wondered. Free from the agony of wanting his love and knowing she no longer received it? Free from the torture of wondering what he and Paula did when they were alone? Free from the pain of a broken heart?

"Yes. Yes! *Yes!*" The admission rose to a crescendo of emotion as her head moved insanely from side to side in denial.

His grip tightened on her arms, cutting off the circulation until the rest of her arm throbbed with pain. Then his hold loosened and he shifted back on his crutches. Stacy buried her face in her numbed hands to smother the sobs that racked her chest.

"I told you I would never let you go." His voice was ominously low, rumbling like thunder in the storm-charged seconds. "But I'm destroying both of us doing that. My father was right when he sent my mother away. Why

ruin two lives? You're free, Stacy. I won't hold
you here.''

"Wh-what are you saying?" She raised her
tear-wet lashes, trying to read the granite-hard
lines of his expression.

"I'm saying that you're free," Cord repeated coldly. "You may leave whenever you
want. Today, tomorrow, this minute, I don't
care.''

With painstaking movement, he pivoted on
his crutches to leave her. Uncertainty plagued
Stacy. Even in her darkest moments she had
never really believed that Cord would send her
away.

His back was to her, broad and strong. With
laborious steps, balanced by his crutches, he
began walking toward the study. Stacy
couldn't let him go without knowing for sure
what he meant.

Her fingers touched his arm to detain him.
He stopped immediately, his muscles stiffening beneath her hand, but he didn't turn to
face her.

"I gave you what you wanted," he growled.
"What is it now?"

"I—I . . ." she faltered at the aloof profile
she saw. "I want to know if it's what you
want."

His jaw clenched for an instant. "Stacy, you're free to do what you want. You can go or stay. But don't make me look at you again."

Her hand fell away from his arm, the nails digging into the palms. Stacy lifted her chin with a false attempt to react with dignity to his final, cutting statement.

"Tell—tell Maria to pack my things," she said numbly. "I'll let her know where I want them to be sent."

"I will," he agreed tersely, and began walking toward the study again.

Stacy watched him for a painful second, then pivoted to race back up the stairs. She threw a few essential items into an overnight bag and hurried out of the room. Cord had made no reference to Josh and neither had she. She was leaving, but she was taking Josh with her.

In his room, she quickly added his things to her case. When it was locked and sitting beside the door, she walked to the bed to wake the slumbering boy.

He rubbed his eyes sleepily when she shook his shoulders. "I'm tired," he grumbled.

"You have to get up now," she coaxed, lifting him to a sitting position. "We're leaving."

The statement gained his immediate interest. "Where are we going?"

Stacy hesitated. This was not the time to tell him the truth, not when she wanted to get him out of the house without Cord being aware of what she was doing. She tucked the tails of his shirt into his pants.

"We're going on a trip." It was a half-truth.

"Where?"

Stacy had no idea. It didn't seem to matter where they went. "You'll see." She tried to make it sound like a mysterious adventure.

Taking Josh by the hand, she hurried down the stairs, carrying the suitcase. Silence came from the study. She didn't know if Cord was there or not and she didn't pause to find out.

Outside, Josh gave her a confused look. "Isn't daddy coming with us?"

"Not this time." Her throat constricted and she bustled him into the car.

Stacy didn't look back at the house as she reversed the car out of the driveway onto the lane. She didn't dare or she wouldn't have the strength to leave.

Chaos reigned over her thoughts, scattering them to the winds and leaving her without conscious direction. Road dust billowed from the accelerating car tires. She drove in a daze, not knowing or caring where she was going. Her eyes were dry, parched by pain that was beyond tears. Staring straight ahead, her mind registered nothing that she saw. She wasn't even aware when the car stopped.

"Mommy, why are we stopping here?" Josh laid a hand on her shoulder. Her hands were still gripping the steering wheel as she tried to shake off the stupor that paralyzed her. "Mommy, why have we come to Mary's house? Aren't we going on a trip?"

Mary's house. The words pierced the fog. With an effort Stacy focused her gaze on the familiar ranch-style home of Mary Buchanan. Something inside her began to crumble. It suddenly became imperative that she reach her best friend before that 'something' caved in.

"Come on, Josh." She switched off the engine and stepped out of the car.

Indifferent to her son's bewilderment as he scrambled out, Stacy walked robotlike to the front door and rang the bell. A few seconds later it was opened and Mary's smiling face greeted them.

"Stacy, this is a surprise!" the redhead exclaimed in delight, swinging the door open wider. "Come in. You'll have to excuse the house. It's a mess, but I'm in the middle of—''

Stacy's grip tightened on Josh's hand. "Can you put us up?'' There was a ring of despair in her voice as she interrupted.

Astonishment opened Mary's mouth. "Well, of course, but—''

"I've left Cord," Stacy answered the question that had been forming in her friend's mind.

"You've what?" Mary exclaimed incredulously. "Stacy, you can't mean it! Why, for heaven's sake?''

There was a shuddering collapse within. A black void swirled in front of Stacy's eyes. She didn't have to answer the question as she slipped into unconsciousness.

The dark world wrapped her in a protective cocoon, insulating her mind from the pain it couldn't bear. Occasionally a haunting image of Cord would drift into the blackness. Her lips would form his name and she would call out to him. The masculine vision would look at her with silent contempt and fade away.

The last time his ghost appeared, he took her hand and looked at her gravely. "I'll always be with you, Stacy," the image told her. "I'll never leave you.''

"No! No!" She protested the bitterness of her fate that she should always be haunted by his ghost.

"Shh, darling," the familiar voice soothed. "You must rest."

Then the apparition dissolved into a mist, and oblivion claimed her again. She welcomed the black void, seeking its darkest corner to escape from Cord's specter.

For a long time Stacy remained safe in her vacuum, untouched by outside forces. Then a hand took her arm and lifted it, almost physically drawing her back into reality. Her lashes fluttered in protest, resisting the attempt to bring her back to the world she couldn't endure without Cord.

"Have you decided to rejoin us Stacy?" a familiar voice inquired gently.

A frown creased her forehead. It wasn't Cord's voice that spoke to her. Nor was it Cord's patrician features Stacy saw when she was finally able to focus her gaze on the man standing beside her. The stocky figure belonged to Bill Buchanan. She stared at him bewilderedly for a minute, as he held her wrist in his fingers, checking her pulse.

"Wh-what happened?" she murmured in a disoriented fashion. Was she ill?

"You collapsed," the doctor informed her with a faint smile, "as I predicted you would if you didn't get away for a while." With her pulse taken, he let her arm lie back along her side.

"I don't understand," Stacy murmured with a confused shake of her had.

"It was a case of complete exhaustion," he explained. "When you wouldn't give your body the rest it needed, it took over. That's why you blacked out."

A movement near the window caught Stacy's eye, and her pulse rocked at the sight of Cord leaning on his crutches. Sunlight streamed over his shoulder, blinding her to the expression on his handsome face.

"What are you doing here?" she breathed, her heart fluctuating between fear and hope.

Bill Buchanan glanced from Stacy to Cord. "I'll leave you alone for a few minutes." He addressed the statement to Cord. "Only for a few minutes, though. She still needs a lot of rest."

There was a curt nod of agreement from Cord, followed by silence as the doctor withdrew from the room. Stacy's gaze searched the hidden recesses of his patrician features.

"Why are you here?" Stacy repeated. Instantly the answer occurred to her. "You've come to take Josh, haven't you?" She thought that subconsciously she had known that Cord would come after their son. "That's why you've come, isn't it?" Pain throbbed in her voice.

Cord moved out of the sunlight. His expression was an inscrutable mask that told her nothing. He stopped beside the bed.

"Mary phoned to let me know what happened. I am still your husband," he inserted dryly. "I came because I wanted to make sure you were all right."

Stacy turned her head away.

"What difference would it make to you?" she muttered in self-pity.

"I haven't stopped caring about you, Stacy," he declared with a hiss of impatience.

No, she supposed he hadn't. He might have stopped loving her, but they had shared too many things for him to stop caring. A broken sigh quivered from her lungs.

"You won't take Josh, will you?" she asked weakly.

Cord exhaled heavily. "No, I won't take Josh." He seemed to hesitate. "You're going to need rest. You're welcome to come back to the ranch until you're better."

"I won't go back there!" Stacy violently rejected the suggestion and its implication of further torment at seeing Cord and Paula together.

"Very well," he nodded grimly, and turned on his crutches. "I have to be getting back to the ranch. There are a lot of things to be done."

"Yes." There was a poignant catch in her voice. "The horse sale is tomorrow, isn't it?"

Cord paused, not quite looking over his shoulder.

"You've been unconscious for a long time, Stacy. Tomorrow is today. The auction is going on right now."

Had she been unconscious that long? The discovery startled her.

"I'll see you later," he offered distantly and opened the bedroom door.

"No," Stacy responded abruptly. His concern for her welfare was not enough when she hungered for his love. "There's no need for you to come back," she added stiffly.

His shoulders squared slightly. "Perhaps not," was his noncommittal response. "I'll let

Josh know you're okay. He's been worried.'' He moved out of the room.

The door closed and Stacy turned her face into the pillow. Shutting her eyes tightly, she held back the tears. Rest, Bill Buchanan had decreed. It seemed an impossible order. Yet within minutes, her exhausted body had induced sleep.

The opening of the door awakened her. Through half-closed eyes, she glanced at the visitor, not welcoming the interruption from her heavy sleep. At least in sleep she stopped thinking and feeling. When her gaze focused on Paula, she was even less glad.

''How are you feeling?'' Paula smiled sympathetically.

Stacy ignored the question. ''Why are you here?'' To rub salt into the wounds, she added silently in resentment.

''I brought some things for Josh,'' the blonde explained. ''I thought I'd look in to see how you were while I was here.''

''I'm fine.'' Stacy breathed tightly, raking the fingers of one hand through the sides of her hair. ''Please go away. You've done enough damage already.'' Bitterness surfaced with a rush that she couldn't hold back. ''Unless you've come to gloat over your victory.''

Frowning, Paula exhaled a confused laugh. "What on earth are you talking about?"

"Stop the pretense, Paula." Her voice was strangled with emotion. "You know very well that I'm talking about Cord. To the victor belong the spoils. I've conceded that you're the victor. Now get out of here!"

A charged moment of silence followed Stacy's choked outburst. Then Paula advanced into the room, her blue eyes narrowing.

"I don't like what you're saying, Stacy. Mary told me some nonsense about you telling her you'd left Cord just before you collapsed yesterday. Or was it nonsense?" she accused.

"Hardly." Stacy blinked furiously at her tears, holding them back. "He's all yours now."

"That's wonderful!" Paula exclaimed with dry amusement. "Do you actually mean you left Cord because of me?"

"You surely didn't expect me to stay while the two of you carried on your little affair? I do have some pride left," Stacy declared tautly.

"An affair? Cord and me?" Paula's mouth remained open in astonishment.

"I saw the two of you together." Stacy hated Paula's show of innocence. "Laughing and smiling and sharing your secret jokes."

"The joke is on you, honey." Paula shook her head. "Not that I wouldn't give my eye-teeth to have an affair with your husband, because I would. Two things would stop me, though. One is that I happen to like you. And the second, and overriding reason, is that Cord and I are just friends. If you'll pardon the usage of an oft-used cliché, he regards me as a sister."

"I don't believe you," she said, because she wanted to believe it so desperately.

"Cord is a one-woman man and that one woman is you, Stacy."

"But he said—" Her head spun. Could it be true? "I thought—"

"How much more proof do you need?" Paula sighed. "The poor man never left your side the whole time you were unconscious. Mary said he was a man possessed, sitting beside the bed staring at you."

It hadn't been a dream. Those weren't ghosts and visions of Cord that had haunted her when she was unconscious. It had really been Cord.

"But—" Stacy pressed a hand against her temple in confusion. "Why did he tell me to leave?"

"Probably because he thought that you wanted to go." Paula shrugged. "It certainly wasn't because he'd stopped loving you. In fact, it was probably the reverse. He loved you too much to keep you against your will."

It was all too possible that everything Paula said was true. She had never been able to convince Cord after that argument that she had not grown bored with the ranch and its lifestyle as his mother had done long ago. And he still mistakenly believed that she cared for Travis.

Throwing back the bedcovers, Stacy started to rise. The blackness that suddenly began spinning in front of her sent her reeling back against the pillow. When it receded, she tried to rise again.

"What do you think you're doing?" Paula was at her side, trying to halt her movement. "You're still too weak."

"I have to get to the ranch." Determinedly Stacy tried to sit up. "I have to see Cord."

"I understand that you have to straighten things out, but—"

The bedroom door burst open and Cord came swinging in, barely using his crutches. Joy leaped into Stacy's brown eyes at the sight of him.

"Cord!" she cried out to him, flinging open her arms as Paula discreetly stepped to one side.

He stopped just short of her reach, his dark eyes scanning her face. "I've just been talking to Travis." He glanced over his shoulder at the tall figure standing in the doorway. "He said—"

Stacy guessed what Travis had said. He had obviously cleared up the matter of her supposed affair with him and her fears that Cord had been having one with Paula.

She interrupted him with a laugh. "I've just been talking to Paula."

In the next second he was sitting on the bed, crushing her against his chest. Stacy clung to him without restraint as he buried his face in the curve of her neck.

"It is true, then." His voice was muffled by the bruising kisses he trailed over the column of her throat. "You love me?"

"I love you," she whispered achingly against his ear.

Cord shuddered against her, raising his head to gaze at her upturned face, flushed and animated with her love. A mixture of tender devotion and fiery passion blazed in his dark eyes.

"I never thought it was possible to love you more than I did in the beginning," he murmured for her hearing alone. "But I do, darling."

Rapture quivered through Stacy. Her lips moved inexorably closer to the sensuous line of his mouth, hard and firm.

Their contact was prevented by a third voice dryly inquiring, "What's going on here? A lovers' reunion?"

With a faintly embarrassed start, Stacy moved away from the inviting lips. Her glowing brown eyes swung to Bill Buchanan standing behind his redhaired wife in the doorway. Mary had a tray in her hands.

"It certainly looks that way, doesn't it?" Paula chimed in. "Travis and I were just wondering how we could disappear before it got too warm in here."

"I was bringing you and Stacy some hot tea," Mary smiled at Paula. "I thought it would give Stacy some strength. Obviously she doesn't need it."

Cord smiled at Stacy, stealing her breath with the sheer charm of it.

"Your timing is terrible, Mary." He wrenched his gaze from Stacy. "But since you are here, bring some more cups. I want my wife stronger soon."

"We're intruding," protested Paula. "The two of you should be alone."

"Bill warned me this morning about over-exciting Stacy when she regained consciousness." The intimate light in his eyes danced over the sudden flush in her cheeks. "So I think all of you should stay or I'll forget about his advice."

"We'll stay for a few minutes," Bill agreed. "Long enough to drink to your happiness."

Minutes later they were all lifting their tea cups in a mock toast. As Cord touched the rim of his china cup to Stacy's he gazed into her eyes.

"I'm the luckiest man in the world," he murmured. "To love you and be loved by you with no end in sight."

His head dipped slowly toward hers, drinking from her lips, barely controlling his insatiable thirst. Stacy felt positively weak when he lifted his head. Somehow she raised the tea cup to her mouth and sipped at the reviving liquid, her gaze unable to leave Cord as he did the same, sealing their private toast.

"This should be champagne," Cord declared regretfully.

"Isn't it?" she smiled, giddy from his kiss.

"When you can't tell tea from champagne, you're definitely in love," Bill laughed. His hand slipped under his wife's elbow. "I think it's time we made our exit, Mary."

"Me, too," Paula joined in.

This time Cord didn't protest. Only Travis lingered after the others had left. His hat was in his hand.

"I'll be leaving, too," he said finally when Cord looked expectantly at him. "Now that the quarter-horse auction is over, the ranch work will be back to normal. You and Stacy can handle it."

"You don't mean you're leaving permanently?" Stacy breathed.

"You don't need me anymore." Travis shook his head and smiled.

"But we want you to stay," she protested, glancing at her husband. "Don't we, Cord?"

"Definitely," he agreed.

"Thanks, but—" again there was a negative shake of the dark hair winged with silver tips "—I never planned to stay this long anyway. I started looking for a ranch of my own. It's time I found it."

"Travis, I—" a seriousness entered Cord's expression "—I was wrong about a lot of things that I'm sorry for now. I've never thanked you for all you did for us."

"It isn't necessary. You had your reasons at the time, so there's nothing to forgive. As for thanks, well—" his mouth quirked as he placed the wide-brimmed Stetson on his head "—I've had that today."

"Won't you stay for a few days?" Stacy asked as Travis walked toward the door.

"I don't like prolonged goodbyes," he stated, pausing in the doorway.

"When you buy that ranch," Cord told him, "let us know. I have a seed bull and thirty cows that belong to you."

"That isn't necessary—" Travis began firmly.

"It's a bonus," Cord announced. "Anyone else would have stolen that much from me in a year. Besides, I'm giving you thirty-one head-aches on the hoof!"

The grooves around his mouth deepened as he met Travis's gaze. A smile curved the fore-man's mouth. He raised a finger to his hat brim and walked into the hallway, closing the door behind him.

"That was generous of you, darling," Stacy smiled.

"Generous?" Cord looked at her in a bemused way. "I'd give him my ranch for opening my eyes to the truth—if it didn't already belong to our son."

He took the tea cup from her hand and set it on the bedside table. It left her hand free to lightly caress the powerful line of his jaw.

"Cord," she whispered.

"I've been such a fool about so many things." He caught her fingers and kissed the tips. "Can you ever forgive me for the terrible things I said to you?"

"Of course," Stacy sighed.

"I loved you so much that I couldn't stand the thought of you staying out of pity for a cripple." Cord frowned at the memory of their bitter arguments. "Each time you came near me, I doubted that it was because you loved me. That's why I kept pushing you away, why I kept hurting you and destroying myself each time I succeeded."

Stacy slid her fingers inside his shirt, feeling the warmth of his body heat and the dark hairs tickling the palms of her hands. She tilted her head back, her lips moist and parted.

"Try pushing me away now, darling," she declared huskily.

Beneath her hands, she felt his heartbeat stop for an instant. Then he was pushing her away—back against the pillow as his mouth closed over hers.

"Mommy!" Josh's voice called from the hallway.

Stacy moved in a faint protest beneath his commanding kiss, and Cord smiled against her trembling lips. "Mary will find something for him to do for a little while. She's a married woman."

Sure enough, Stacy heard Mary's voice in the hall, and wound her arms around Cord's neck.

IN FROM
THE COLD

NORA
ROBERTS

Chapter One

His name was MacGregor. He clung to that even as he clung to the horse's reins. The pain was alive, capering down his arm like a dozen dancing devils. Hot, branding, hot, despite the December wind and blowing snow.

He could no longer direct the horse but rode on, trusting her to find her way through the twisting paths made by Indian or deer or white man. He was alone with the scent of snow and pine, the muffled thud of his mount's hooves and the gloom of early twilight. A world hushed by the sea of wind washing through the trees.

Instinct told him he was far from Boston now, far from the crowds, the warm hearths, the civilized. Safe. Perhaps safe. The snow would cover the trail his horse left and the guiding path of his own blood.

But safe wasn't enough for him. It never had been. He was determined to stay alive, and for one fierce reason. A dead man couldn't fight. By all that was holy he had vowed to fight until he was free.

Shivering despite the heavy buckskins and furs, teeth chattering now from a chill that came from within as well as without, he leaned forward to speak to the horse, soothing in Gaelic. His skin was clammy with the heat of the pain, but his blood was like the ice that formed on the bare branches of the trees surrounding him. He could see the mare's breath blow out in white streams as she trudged on through the deepening snow. He prayed as only a man who could feel his own blood pouring out of him could pray. For life.

There was a battle yet to be fought. He'd be damned if he'd die before he'd raised his sword.

The mare gave a sympathetic whinny as he slumped against her neck, his breathing labored. Trouble was in the air, as well as the scent of blood. With a toss of her head, she walked into the wind, following her own instinct for survival and heading west.

The pain was like a dream now, floating in his mind, swimming through his body. He thought if he could only wake, it would disappear. As dreams do. He had other dreams—violent and vivid. To fight the British for all they had stolen from him. To take back his name and his land—to fight for all the MacGregors had held with pride and sweat and blood. All they had lost.

He had been born in war. It seemed just and right that he would die in war.

But not yet. He struggled to rouse himself. Not yet. The fight had only begun.

He forced an image into his mind. A grand one. Men in feathers and buckskins, their faces blackened with burnt cork and lampblack and grease, boarding the ships *Dartmouth*, *Eleanor* and *Beaver*. Ordinary men, he remembered, merchants and craftsmen and students. Some fueled with grog, some with righteousness. The hoisting and smashing of the chests of the damned and detested tea. The satisfying splash as broken crates of it hit the cold water of Boston Harbor at Griffin's Wharf. He remembered how disgorged chests had been heaped up in the muck of low tide like stacks of hay.

So large a cup of tea for the fishes, he thought now. Aye, they had been merry, but purposeful. Determined. United. They would need to be all of those things to fight and win the war that so many didn't understand had already begun.

How long had it been since that glorious night? One day? Two? It had been his bad luck that he had run into two drunk and edgy redcoats as dawn had been breaking. They knew him. His face, his name, his politics were well-known in Boston. He'd done nothing to endear himself to the British militia.

Perhaps they had only meant to harass and bully him a bit. Perhaps they hadn't meant to make good their threat to arrest him—on charges they hadn't made clear. But when one had drawn a sword, MacGregor's weapon had all but leaped into his own hand. The fight had been brief—and foolish, he could admit now. He was still unsure if he had killed or only wounded the impetuous soldier. But his comrade had had murder in his eye when he had drawn his weapon.

Though MacGregor had been quick to mount and ride, the musket ball had slammed viciously into his shoulder.

He could feel it now, throbbing against muscle. Though the rest of his body was mercifully numb, he could feel that small and agonizing pinpoint of heat. Then his mind was numb, as well, and he felt nothing.

He woke, painfully. He was lying in the blanket of snow, face up so that he could see dimly the swirl of white flakes against a heavy gray sky. He'd fallen from his horse. He wasn't close enough to death to escape the embarrassment of it. With effort, he pushed himself to his knees. The mare was waiting patiently beside him, eyeing him with a mild sort of surprise.

"I'll trust you to keep this to yourself, lass." It was the weak sound of his own voice that brought him the first trace of fear. Gritting his teeth, he reached for the reins and pulled himself shakily to his feet. "Shelter." He swayed, grayed out and knew he could never find the strength to mount. Holding tight, he clucked to the mare and let her pull his weary body along.

Step after step he fought the urge to collapse and let the cold take him. They said there was little pain in freezing to death. Like sleep it was, a cold, painless sleep.

And how the devil did they know unless they'd lived to tell the tale? He laughed at the thought, but the laugh turned to a cough that weakened him.

Time, distance, direction were utterly lost to him. He tried to think of his family, the warmth of them. His parents and brothers and sisters in Scotland. Beloved Scotland, where they fought to keep hope alive. His aunts and uncles and cousins in Virginia, where they worked for the right to a new life in a new land. And he, he was somewhere between, caught between his love of the old and his fascination with the new.

But in either land, there was one common enemy. It strengthened him to think of it. The British. Damn them. They had proscribed his name and butchered his people. Now they were reaching their greedy hands across the ocean so that the half-mad English king could impose his bloody laws and collect his bloody taxes.

He stumbled, and his hold on the reins nearly broke. For a moment he rested, his head against the mare's neck, his eyes closed. His father's face seemed to float into his mind, his eyes still bright with pride.

"Make a place for yourself," he'd told his son. "Never forget, you're a MacGregor."

No, he wouldn't forget.

Wearily he opened his eyes. He saw, through the swirling snow, the shape of a building. Cautious, he blinked, rubbed his tired eyes with his free hand. Still the shape remained, gray and indistinct, but real.

"Well, lass." He leaned heavily against his horse. "Perhaps this isn't the day to die after all."

Step by step he trudged toward it. It was a barn, a large one, well built of pine logs. His numb fingers fumbled with the latch. His knees threatened to buckle. Then he was inside, with the smell and the blessed heat of animals.

It was dark. He moved by instinct to a mound of hay in the stall of a brindled cow. The bovine lady objected with a nervous moo.

It was the last sound he heard.

Alanna pulled on her woolen cape. The fire in the kitchen hearth burned brightly and smelled faintly, cheerfully, of apple logs. It was a small thing, a normal thing, but it pleased her. She'd woken in a mood of happy anticipation. It was the snow, she imagined, though her father had risen from his bed cursing it. She loved the purity of it, the way it clung to the bare branches of trees her father and brothers had yet to clear.

It was already slowing, and within the hour the barnyard would be tracked with footprints, hers included. There were animals to tend to, eggs to gather, harnesses to repair and wood to chop. But for now, for just a moment, she looked out the small window and enjoyed.

If her father caught her at it, he would shake his head and call her a dreamer. It would be said roughly—not with anger, she thought, but with regret. Her mother had been a dreamer, but she had died before her dream of a home and land and plenty had been fully realized.

Cyrus Murphy wasn't a hard man, Alanna thought now. He never had been. It had been death, too many deaths, that had caused him to become rough and prickly. Two bairns, and later, their beloved mother. Another son, beautiful young Rory, lost in the war against the French.

Her own husband, Alanna mused, sweet Michael Flynn, taken in a less dramatic way but taken nonetheless.

She didn't often think of Michael. After all, she had been three months a wife and three years a widow. But he had been a kind man and a good one, and she regretted bitterly that they had never had the chance to make a family.

But today wasn't a day for old sorrows, she reminded herself. Pulling up the hood of her cape, she stepped outside. Today was a day for promises, for beginnings. Christmas was coming fast. She was determined to make it a joyful one.

Already she'd spent hours at her spinning wheel and loom. There were new mufflers and mittens and caps for her brothers. Blue for Johnny and red for Brian. For her father she had painted a miniature of her mother. And had paid the local silversmith a lot of pennies for a frame.

She knew her choices would please. Just as the meal she had planned for their Christmas feast would please. It was all that mattered to her—keeping her family together and happy and safe.

The door of the barn was unlatched. With a sound of annoyance, she pulled it to behind her. It was a good thing she had found it so, she thought, rather than her father, or her young brother, Brian, would have earned the raw side of his tongue.

As she stepped inside the barn, she shook her hood back and reached automatically for the wooden buckets that hung beside the door.

Because there was little light she took a lamp,
lighting it carefully.

By the time she had finished the milking,
Brian and Johnny would come to feed the
stock and clean the stalls. Then she would
gather the eggs and fix her men a hearty
breakfast.

She started to hum as she walked down the
wide aisle in the center of the barn. Then she
stopped dead as she spotted the roan mare
standing slack hipped and weary beside the
cow stall.

"Sweet Jesus." She put a hand to her heart
as it lurched. The mare blew a greeting and
shifted.

If there was a horse, there was a rider. At
twenty, Alanna wasn't young enough or naive
enough to believe all travelers were friendly
and meant no harm to a woman alone. She
could have turned and run, sent up a shout for
her father and brothers. But though she had
taken Michael Flynn's name, she was born a
Murphy. A Murphy protected his own.

Head up, she started forward. "I'll have
your name and your business," she said. Only
the horse answered her. When she was close
enough she touched the mare on her nose.
"What kind of a master have you who leaves

you standing wet and saddled?'' Incensed for the horse's sake, she set down her buckets and raised her voice. "All right, come out with you. It's Murphy land you're on.''

The cows mooed.

With a hand on her hip, she looked around. "No one's begrudging you shelter from the storm,'' she continued. "Or a decent breakfast, for that matter. But I'll have a word with you for leaving your horse so.''

When there was still no answer, her temper rose. Muttering, she began to uncinch the saddle herself. And nearly tripped over a pair of boots.

Fine boots at that, she thought, staring down at them. They poked out of the cow stall, their good brown leather dulled with snow and mud. She stepped quietly closer to see them attached to a pair of long, muscled legs in worn buckskin.

Sure and there was a yard of them, she thought, nibbling on her lip. And gloriously masculine in the loose-fitting breeches. Creeping closer, she saw hips, lean, a narrow waist belted with leather and a torso covered with a long doublet and a fur wrap.

A finer figure of a man she couldn't remember seeing. And since he'd chosen her barn to sleep, she found it only right that she look her fill. He was a big one, she decided, tilting her head and holding the lamp higher. Taller than either of her brothers. She leaned closer, wanting to see the rest of him.

His hair was dark. Not brown, she realized, as she narrowed her eyes, but deep red, like Brian's chestnut gelding. He wore no beard, but there was stubble on his chin and around his full, handsome mouth. Aye, handsome, she decided with feminine appreciation. A strong, bony face, aristocratic somehow, with its high brow and chiseled features.

The kind of face a woman's heart would flutter over, she was sure. But she wasn't interested in fluttering or flirting. She wanted the man up and out of her way so that she could get to her milking.

"Sir." She nudged his boot with the toe of hers. No response. Setting her hands on her hips, she decided he was drunk as a lord. What else was there that caused a man to sleep as though dead? "Wake up, you sod. I can't milk around you." She kicked him, none too gently, in the leg and got only a faint groan for an answer. "All right, boy-o." She bent down to give him a good shake. She was prepared for the stench of liquor but instead caught the coppery odor of blood.

Anger forgotten, she knelt down to carefully push aside the thick fur over his shoulders. She sucked in a breath as she saw the long stain along his shirtfront. Her fingers were wet with his blood as she felt for a pulse.

"Well, you're still alive," she murmured. "With God's will and a bit of luck we might keep you that way."

Before she could rise to call her brothers, his hand clamped over her wrist. His eyes were open now, she saw. They were green, with just a hint of blue. Like the sea. But there was pain in them. Compassion had her leaning closer to offer comfort.

Then her hand plunged deep into the hay as he tugged her off balance so that she was all but lying on him. She had the quick impression of a firm body and raging heat. Her sound of indignation was muffled against his lips. The kiss was brief but surprisingly firm before his head fell back again. He gave her a quick, cocky smile.

"Well, I'm not dead anyway. Lips like yours would have no place in hell."

As compliments went, she'd had better. Before she could tell him so, he fainted.

Six exciting series for you every month... from Harlequin

HARLEQUIN
Romance®

The series that started it all

Tender, captivating and heartwarming...
love stories that sweep you off to faraway places
and delight you with the magic of love.

◆

Harlequin Presents®

Powerful contemporary love stories...as individual as the women who read them

The No. 1 romance series...
exciting love stories for you, the woman of today...
a rare blend of passion and dramatic realism.

◆

Harlequin Superromance®

It's more than romance... it's Harlequin Superromance

A sophisticated, contemporary romance-fiction
series, providing you with a longer,
more involving read...a richer mix of complex plots,
realism and adventure.

H A R L E Q U I N
American Romance®
Harlequin celebrates the American woman...

...by offering you romance stories written about American women, by American women for American women. This series offers you contemporary romances uniquely North American in flavor and appeal.

◆

H A R L E Q U I N
Temptation®

Passionate stories for today's woman

An exciting series of sensual, mature stories of love...dilemmas, choices, resolutions... all contemporary issues dealt with in a true-to-life fashion by some of your favorite authors.

◆

Harlequin Intrigue®
Because romance can be quite an adventure

Harlequin Intrigue, an innovative series that blends the romance you expect... with the unexpected. Each story has an added element of intrigue that provides a new twist to the Harlequin tradition of romance excellence.

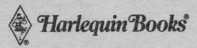 *Harlequin Books*®

PROD-A-2R

AVAILABLE NOW

DREAMSCAPE
Harlequin
ROMANCE
TM

This month, two worlds will collide in four very special romance titles. Somewhere between first meeting and happy ending, Dreamscape Romance will sweep you to the very edge of reality where everyday reason cannot conquer unlimited imagination—or the power of love. The timeless mysteries of reincarnation, telepathy, psychic visions and earthbound spirits intensify the modern lives and passion of ordinary men and women with an extraordinary alluring force.

Available now!

EARTHBOUND—Rebecca Flanders
THIS TIME FOREVER—Margaret Chittenden
MOONSPELL—Regan Forest
PRINCE OF DREAMS—Carly Bishop

DRSC-R